TALK—OR ELSE . . .

"Hello there," came a voice from behind him. "My name is Remo and you're going to talk to me. You've caused me a problem. You're going to uncause it. How did you kill Kaufmann? Who did it for you?"

"My wrist. I can't talk."

"I left you your throat to talk. Now if you're not going to use it for me, I'll take it with me."

"There's a man—he provides the service. Special killings are contracted out. It's expensive—a hundred thousand in advance."

When Remo left, Polastro picked up the phone. "Look," he said. "I'm going to talk. This is an open line so ask questions at the end. Both my wrists are broken. I've lost two of my best men. There is a man after you. He must use some kind of weird killing machine. I gave him your name. I had to. He would have killed me. But you can stop him."

"If it's who I think it is—no one can stop him!" The phone went dead.

The Destroyer Series:

The Destroyer

CHILD'S PLAY #23

by Richard Sapir & Warren Murphy

PINNACLE BOOKS • NEW YORK CITY

This is a work of fiction. All the characters and events portrayed in this book are fictional, and any resemblance to real people or incidents is purely coincidental.

THE DESTROYER: CHILD'S PLAY

An original Pinnacle Books edition, published for the first time anywhere.

ISBN: 0-523-00842-2

First printing, April 1976

Cover illustration by Hector Garrido

Printed in the United States of America

PINNACLE BOOKS, INC.
275 Madison Avenue
New York, N.Y. 10016

For Megan

CHILD'S PLAY

CHAPTER ONE

The left arm came sailing over the schoolyard
fence ... without a body on it. The left leg skittered into a sandbox, where the blood pumped out
of the thigh stump and onto a rubber play shovel.
There were no sharp edges on this yellow shovel
the size of a large serving spoon because it was
guaranteed by the National Parental Council as
"child safe." In the playground of the Fairview,
Oklahoma, Country Day School there was also no
left side of Robert Calder.

Jimmy Wilkes and Katherine Poffer remembered that was the side on which Mr. Calder had
been holding the "froobie."

"Tell the men what a froobie is, Katherine,"
said the nurse in the infirmary of the Fairview
Country Day School as two men in polished cor-
dovan shoes and neat gray suits with white shirts
and striped ties took notes on a small tape re-

corder. They had told the Fairview County Sheriff's office they wanted to talk to the children first, and afterward the sheriff could get all the information he needed. He had complained that homicide was not a federal crime but a state crime, and if the Justice Department wanted the assistance of the Fairview County Sheriff's Office, they should tell him what the hell was up. Especially since November was four months away and while *they* had assured jobs, an elected county official sure as hell didn't, and one hand washes the other if the FBI knew what the Fairview County Sheriff's office meant. They did, and they didn't want him talking to the children first.

So Katherine Poffer, seven, explained to the two FBI agents what a froobie was.

"It's nice," said Kathy.

"Tell them what it does, dear," said the nurse.

"It's like a frisbee. It's plastic, only it squiggles if you get it right," said Jimmy Wilkes, six.

"She said me. She said I should say what a froobie is," said Katherine Poffer. "It's like a frisbee only it squiggles," Kathy said with righteous triumph.

"Now when did the bang happen?" asked one of the agents.

"Me or Jimmy?" said Katherine Poffer.

"Either one," said the agent.

"When he threw it, sort of," said Jimmy.

"Sort of?"

"Yeah. Like the froobie was up at his ear, like a quarterback ready to throw."

"Yes," said the agent.

"He was left-handed," said Jimmy Wilkes.

"Yes."

2

"And then, wow, boom," said Jimmy, his hands going out to show a big explosion.

"You didn't see half of him at all," said Katherine Poffer.

"A leg went in the sandbox, and there's no going in the sandbox during afternoon recess," said Jimmy.

"Did you see who brought the froobie to the schoolyard?"

"Nobody brought it. It was there," said Jimmy.

"Somebody must have brought it," said the agent.

"The new boy maybe brought it," said Katherine.

"Some grownup," said the agent. "Was any grownup standing near the schoolyard?"

"The ice cream man for a while," said Jimmy. The two agents went on with the interview. They had talked to the ice cream vendor already, and he had seen nothing. He was also not the kind of person to withhold information. This wasn't Brooklyn, where people stuck their noses behind doors and kept them there for their safety. This was heartland America, where if a strange dog wandered into town, everyone knew and was willing not only to talk about it but to tell you if it was a Communist dog or a Mafia dog. This was pin-clean small-town USA, where everyone not only knew everyone else but talked about everyone else. And no one knew who had killed Mr. Calder and while everyone was downright glad to cooperate with the FBI—"We're on your side, fellas"—no one knew who had planted the bomb. And what was the FBI doing here in Fairview

3

anyway? This wasn't a federal crime, you know. Was Mr. Calder a secret spy?

No, ma'am.

Was he a secret scientist?

No, sir.

Was he a big Mafia *cappucino* who split with the family?

No, sir.

Was he a hit? He was a real live hit, wasn't he?

Well, ma'am, we believe that his demise was, so to speak, intentional.

That's for dang sure. Folks don't blow up by accident.

Yes, sir.

So here they were, talking to little children about froobies and bang bangs and sand boxes, while other agents went around picking up pieces of the man called Calder from the schoolyard.

"Anything else?" said the agent.

"He went like a ladyfinger. Bang. You know how ladyfingers blow up when you light them," said Jimmy.

"Ladyfingers are firecrackers. They're against the law. I never used them," said Kathy Poffer. "Jimmy used them a lot though. Jimmy and Johnny Kruse and Irene Blasinips. She showed herself to the boys, too. I know that."

"And you took extra cookies before nap," said Jimmy, turning in his playmate to the FBI. But the FBI did not seem interested in firecrackers or who showed what to whom, just Mr. Calder who was new to the town and had gone bang like a ladyfinger with some of him left, like those little firecrackers that never quite went all up.

There was something else, too, Jimmy remem-

4

bered, but no one would be interested in that. They wanted to know about the bang, not about the new kid who wouldn't let anyone play with the froobie but just hung around sort of, and when Mr. Calder came by, called out to him and seemed to know him because he called him Mr. Calder.

"Mr. Calder, they say you can throw a football, but I bet you can't throw a froobie," the new kid had said.

And everyone had watched Mr. Calder take the froobie, while the new kid had backed away to the other side of the schoolyard as Mr. Calder raised the yellow plastic froobie to his ear, just like the football players did when they wanted to throw footballs like grownups. But when the froobie was ready to go, *bang*.

And Mr. Calder was only partly left. Outside the infirmary, the strangers were still examining the area for the sprayed pieces of Mr. Calder. Lights came on, and there were television cameras, and everyone was talking about how hard it must have been on Jimmy and Kathy to see such a horrible thing at their ages, so Kathy started to cry, and since Kathy was crying and everyone said it was horrible and since Jimmy's mother was hugging him as if something horrible had happened, Jimmy started to cry, too.

"The poor babies," said someone, and Jimmy couldn't stop crying. All this over Mr. Calder, who went up like a little firecracker with some of him left.

The two agents caught the nightly news on television as they went over their day's notes. There were the two children, crying away before the tel-

evision cameras. The schoolyard. And Calder's home.

"A modest home on a well-kept street," said the announcer of the local television station.

"Well kept, you can bet," said the agent who had questioned the children. "We had both sides and the front of the house covered. And the backyard neighbor was a retired Marine." He blew air out of his mouth and went over the notes. Somehow, apparently in the children's toy, a bomb had been smuggled in. But then why did Calder play with it? How had it happened that a child hadn't grabbed it first and blown himself up, instead of Calder?

How did anyone even know the subject was in Fairview? He had changed his name to Calder when his children were only babies, so they never knew his real name. No one at the factory where he was assistant purchasing agent knew his name. The agent at the plant had kept an eye on that.

No stranger had entered Fairview. No stranger could have entered Fairview without the whole town knowing about it—that was why Fairview had been chosen. Everyone in this town talked. Gossip was the major industry here. That, and the single manufacturing plant.

The agent in charge of the investigation had also been in charge of picking the town for Calder. He had been careful about it. As the district director had told him, keeping the man called Calder alive was a career move:

"If he lives, you have one."

That blunt. That final.

Calder was just one of seven hundred government witnesses hidden away each year by the

Justice Department. Seven hundred. Not one in the last ten years had been uncovered until he was ready for trial. This was necessary because as the Justice Department closed in on the mobs around the country, the mobs had started to fight back in their traditional way.

Good lawyers could occasionally discredit a witness in a courtroom, but the mobs had long ago found out that the best way to get rid of a troublesome witness was simply to *get rid* of him. During the twenties, a government witness against a racketeer signed his death warrant when he signed a statement. A secretary, a witness to a shooting, a thug who wanted to turn state's evidence—the mob would get them, even in jail. And righteously, defense counsel would get the signed statement thrown out of court because the witness's death had denied him his right to cross-examine.

So about ten years ago, the Justice Department had a good idea. Why not give the witnesses new identities and new lives and keep them absolutely secure until the trial? Then, after the trial, give them another life and watch them a while to make sure they were safe? And it had worked. Because now witnesses knew they could testify and live.

So the man called Calder had thought.

The phone in the motel room where the agent was staying rang. It was the district director of the FBI.

The agent wanted to speak first.

"As soon as I finish my report, you can have my resignation."

"Your resignation won't be required."

7

"Don't give me the official bullshit. I know I'm going to Anchorage or somewhere I can't live because of this thing."

"You don't know that. We don't know it. I don't know it. Just continue your work."

"You can't tell me that the agent who loses the first government witness in ten frigging years isn't going to get canned. C'mon, I'm not Bo Peep."

"You're also not the first. We lost two others this morning," said the District Director. "This whole thing may be coming apart."

In a sanitarium called Folcroft on Long Island Sound, giant computers received the details of the Fairview incident and the two others. Because of the designs of these machines, the printouts could only be gotten at one office. It had one-way windows, a large sparse desk, and a terminal which could be operated only through a code. The Fairview incident was the last to clack out of the machine. A gaunt man with a lemony face read all three reports. Unlike the district director in Oklahoma, Dr. Harold W. Smith did not *think* ten years work might be falling apart. He knew it was.

CHAPTER TWO

His name was Remo and the hotel guest wouldn't let him go. Was Remo aware that he and his Oriental friend probably produced an incredible amount of Theta waves and functioned to a great degree at the Alpha level?

Remo didn't know that. Would the guest please pass the salt?

The guest was sure that Remo and his elderly Oriental friend functioned at these states, otherwise how could Remo explain yesterday. How?

The salt.

Certainly, the salt. There was no other explanation, said Dr. Charlese, Averill N., as in Averill Harriman except he wasn't related to the wealthy and famous railroad family, just a poor parapsychologist trying to let people know of the great powers locked within humanity. He had a card:

Dr. Averill N. Charlese
President
Mind Potential Institute
Houston, Texas

He had come down to Mexico City, where the
America Games were now being held, to prove his
theory. Not that it really needed proving, because
it was a fact. Fact. People producing Theta waves
could perform what appeared to be incredible
feats.

Remo suddenly saw a small chart cover his
breakfast of white rice and water. There, in blue
and red and green and yellow, was an ascending
"rainbow." Yellow, at the top, was the conscious
level of the mind, and darkest blue was the deep
Theta state.

Remo looked around for a waiter at the El Conquistador, a large modern hotel built like a simu-
lated Aztec temple, with waiters in Aztec-type
print smocks, surrounded by very un-Aztec
Muzak.

"If I'm bothering you, let me know," said Dr.
Charlese, a pudgy man in his mid-thirties, with a
crown of brownish gold hair gleaming like a helmet fashioned by hot comb and lacquer.

"You're bothering me," said Remo, who folded
the chart and put it in Charlese's gold plaid
jacket.

"Good. Honesty is the basis for a good relationship."

Remo chewed a few kernels of rice until they
were liquid, then he drank it into his stomach. He
eyed a roast beef, sliced thick and fatty and red,
being served at a neighboring table. It had been a
long time since he had had a piece of meat, and

his memory hungered for it. Not his body, which now dictated what he would eat. He remembered that the roast beef used to be good. But that was a long time ago.

"I knew yesterday you were something special," said Dr. Charlese.

Remo tried to remember an incident the day before that might have inflicted this lacquer-headed sparkler of positive thought on him. He could not. There was nothing special the day before, just resting, getting sun and, of course, the training. But Charlese couldn't have been able to tell the training from a nap. Which was what it appeared to be, because at Remo's level of competence, his body had long ago achieved its maximum. He was now working in the limitless frontiers of his mind. Anything more he would learn to do, he would learn in his mind, not in his body.

Charlese opened the chart again, and moved the rice away, explaining that this was his only chart and he didn't want to get food on it.

Remo smiled politely, took the offered chart and, starting at the top left corner, tore it diagonally across. Then he tore the two remaining pieces into four, then the four into eight. He put them in Dr. Charlese's open mouth.

"Fantastic," said Dr. Charlese, spitting the confetti of his chart. A corner with a blue Theta on it landed in the center of Remo's rice. Enough. He rose from the table. He was a thin man, about six feet tall, give or take an inch, depending on how he used his body that day, with high cheekbones and eyes that had a central darkness of limitless, weightless space. He wore gray slacks and a dark turtleneck shirt. His shoes were loafers. As he left

11

the table, the eyes of several women followed him. One sent back a green and yellow Montezuma parfait when she looked at her husband after looking at Remo.

Dr. Charlese followed him.

"You probably don't even remember what you did yesterday," said Dr. Charlese. "You were by the pool."

"Leave," said Remo.

Dr. Charlese followed him to the elevator. Remo waited until the door was just closing before he entered. The elevator was a local, making several stops before the fourteenth floor. When it reached the floor, Dr. Charlese was there smiling.

"Positive thinking. Positive thinking," he said. "I projected my elevator not to make stops."

"Did you do your projecting while standing in front of the buttons?"

"Well, as a matter of fact, yes," said Dr. Charlese. "But it never hurts to help the projection of a positive image. A human being can do whatever he imagines he can do. If you can imagine it, you can do it."

"I'm imagining that you're leaving me alone," said Remo.

"But my imagination is stronger, and I'm imagining that you're going to answer my questions."

"And I'm imagining that you're lying on the carpeting of this hallway with your mouth a mess of broken teeth so you cannot ask questions."

Dr. Charlese thought this quite humorous, because he was imagining Remo telling him the secrets of his power. Remo smiled slightly and was about to show Dr. Charlese how a snapping right hand could overcome any thought, when Dr.

12

Charlese said something that made Remo stop, made him want to know about this man's theories.

"Breathing is the key," said Dr. Charlese. "I know that. Breathing is the whole key to control of those vast reaches of your mind. Did you know that the chart I gave you was nylon mesh? No one could tear it with his hands."

"Would you explain what you're talking about?"

"I had only one copy of that chart. I carried it with me. I didn't want it destroyed so I had it hand-painted on strong nylon mesh, reinforced with steel strands. Something like a steel-belted tire. And you tore it up like it was paper."

"I'm trying to piece this thing together. What do you know about breathing?" Remo asked.

"Yesterday, I saw you by the pool. With the Japanese man."

"Korean. Never call him Japanese," said Remo.

"And I saw you do it. I timed it."

"What? Nobody can tell when I'm exercising."

"Your diaphragm gave you away."

"How?"

"It didn't move. I watched your breathing slow down and then your diaphragm didn't move. Not for twenty-two minutes and fifteen seconds. I have a stopwatch. I time everything."

"Can we talk somewhere privately?"

"I've been sort of evicted from my room. But I'm projecting that someone else will pay the bill."

"No, no. I'm not interested in your projecting. I want to know about breathing," said Remo.

"I knew you could tear that chart when I saw your breathing control."

"Wait," said Remo. "Not out here in the hall." He led Dr. Charlese to his suite. He opened the door quietly and put a finger over his lips. A frail Oriental, with a wisp of a white beard and strands of white hair surrounding his otherwise bald head, sat in a chartreuse kimono, mumbling something. He was watching a television program in which the actors spoke in English. Remo guided Dr. Charlese to another room.

"I didn't know there were American soap operas down here," said Dr. Charlese.

"There aren't. He has them taped specially. Never misses one."

"What was he talking about?"

"It was Korean. He was saying how awful the shows were."

"Then why does he watch them?"

"One never asks why with the Master of Sinanju."

"Who?"

"Never mind. Tell me about breathing."

Dr. Charlese explained: The human brain emitted waves at different levels of consciousness. At the Alpha level, or what they called Alpha waves, people were more relaxed and creative and even exhibited powers of extrasensory perception. At the deeper level, where people emitted what were called Theta waves, people could perform extraordinary feats. This was documented. How many times, for example, had Remo heard of a child trapped underneath a car and the mother lifting that car in a sense of calm purpose? How many times had Remo heard of people fleeing danger

14

and leaping over fences to do so, leaps that would have been Olympic records? How many times had Remo heard of a person surviving a fall, while others in the fall were killed? What were those greater powers?

"Get back to the breathing," said Remo. "What does breathing have to do with these things?"

"That's how we discovered that human beings can produce these waves at will. It's a relaxed breathing process in which you slow down your breathing. You relax your way to power."

"And you can do these things?"

"Well, not exactly me. But I've seen others. You see, I'm not exactly a representative of the institute, anymore. They're very finicky."

"About what?"

"Commissions and things, and using this power for good, I say power is power and has no purpose other than itself."

"You stole money or something?"

"There was an accident. They blamed me for the girl's death, but I say what is the life of a child when I can help all mankind. I, Dr. Averill Charlese. And, with you, we could make a fortune."

"Breathing, you say, huh?"

"Breathing."

And Remo listened. About the institute. About the narrow-minded people running it and how Dr. Charlese was not actually a doctor exactly. He was a doctor in the broader sense. One person bestowed the title on another, therefore he was bestowing it on someone he knew was worthy of the title. Himself.

15

"You could call yourself doctor, too," said Charlese.

"Breathing you say," said Remo.

In the late afternoon, Remo heard the set in the lounge of the suite click off. He nodded for Dr. Charlese to follow.

When they entered the lounge, the old Oriental turned his head.

"Little Father," Remo said, "I would like to introduce you to someone very interesting. He is not privy to any secrets of Sinanju. Neither has he been taught by any master. He learned what he knows in an American City called Houston, Texas, from white men."

Chiun's placid eyes moved up and down the lacquer-haired visitor with the bubbling Rotarian smile. He turned away as if someone had pointed out an orange rind. He was not interested.

"Dr. Charlese, I would like you to meet Chiun, the latest Master of Sinanju."

"Pleased to meet you, sir," said Dr. Charlese. He offered a pudgy hand. Chiun did not turn around. Dr. Charlese looked to Remo, confused.

"He says hello a little differently," said Remo, by way of explanation. Chiun's way of saying hello was to not even turn his head as Remo explained some of the things Dr. Charlese had been talking about.

"Breathing," Remo said. "Nothing mysterious. Nothing great. Just good old American science. By white men."

Chiun chuckled. "Am I now led to believe the awesome magnificence of the Glorious House of Sinanju has been put into a little pill for people?

16

That centuries of discipline and wisdom can be discovered in a test tube?"

"No test tube," said Remo. "Breathing."

"When we talk of breathing, we talk of approaching the unity which makes you a force," Chiun said. "When that man talks of breathing, he means puffing."

"I don't think so, Little Father. I think they may have stumbled onto something. Maybe by accident."

"So glad to meet you, sir. The name's Charlese. Dr. Averill Charlese, no relation to Averill Harriman, the millionaire. And you, sir, are Mr. Chiun?"

Chiun looked off into the blue Mexican sky outside their window.

"He doesn't like to discuss these things with strangers, especially foreigners."

"I'm not foreign. I'm American," said Dr. Charlese. "And so are you."

Remo heard Chiun mumble something in Korean about being able to take whiteness out of the mind but not the soul.

"Go ahead, talk. He's really listening," Remo said. Dr. Charlese began drawing diagrams of the mind on small white cloths he found under an unused ashtray.

Breathing, thought Remo. It had been more than a decade now since he heard that first strange instruction. More than a decade since he had stopped using his body and mind only partially, as other men did.

What appeared to others as great feats of strength and speed were really as effortless to him now as flicking a light switch. As Chiun had

17

said, effort was expended when one functioned improperly. Correctness brought ease.

Remo had been taught that ease when he had been given Sinanju, called Sinanju after the village on the West Korea Bay whence came the Masters of Sinanju. From king to king and emperor to emperor, from pharaoh to Medici, these masters—one or, at most, two-generation—rented their talents and services to the rulers of the world. Assassins whose services paid for the food in the desolate little Korean village where crops did not grow and the fishing was poor. Each Master did not rule the village, but served it, for he was the provider of food.

During many generations their actions were observed by those who would imitate Sinanju. But they only saw, as Chiun had said, the kimono and not the man. They saw the blows when the blows were slow enough for the human eye to see. And from these blows and kicks and the other movements that were slow enough for normal men to see, came karate and ninja and tai kwan do and all that was thought to be the martial arts.

But they were only the rays. Sinanju was the sun source.

And in the travels of the Masters of Sinanju, the current one, Chiun, made contact with an American group that said, "Take this man and teach him things." It had been more than ten years. And it had started with the blows and became the essence—the breathing that now so excited Remo who, since he was born in the west, had always sought to explain Sinanju to himself in Western terms. And always failed.

Maybe Chiun was right: Sinanju could not be

18

explained in terms of the West. Then again, maybe he was wrong.

Remo listened to Dr. Charlese, and although Chiun seemed to be contemplating, Remo knew the Master of Sinanju was taking in every word.

"So you see," said Dr. Charlese in summation. "People are not using their full abilities. More than 90 percent of the human brain is never used. What we do is unlock the human growth potential."

Chiun finally turned and looked at Charlese, whose pudgy pale face was beaded with sweat, even in the air-conditioned chill of the fourteenth-floor Conquistador suite.

"You would see something then?" asked Chiun.

"You betcha," said Dr. Charlese.

Chiun's long fingernails at the end of parched bony hands made a circular signal, calling on Remo for a move.

"That's nothing," Remo said.

"You were the one, Remo, who would invite some passing stranger into the bosom of our home. Then you may demonstrate. And of course I selected a 'nothing.' I did not want you to do it incorrectly."

Remo shrugged. It was a simple exercise. It depended on slowness. You approached the wall with momentum, and then bringing it flat to you so you could practically smell the dust in the ceiling corner, you walked straight up, letting the momentum carry your waist height to the level of your head and then, with your feet just beneath the ceiling, dropping the head down straight to the floor and bringing the feet beneath you just before the head touched. Like so much in the discipline of Sinanju, it appeared to be what it wasn't. The legs only followed the momentum of the body up to the ceiling, though it looked as if you were using them to walk up a wall; it was really only using forward momentum deflected upward by the impact with the wall.

"Golly, wow," said Dr. Charlese. "Wow. Walked right up the frigging wall."

"Well, not exactly," said Remo.

"And you too would do these things?" asked Chiun.

"I'd be rich," said Dr. Charlese. "I could buy off the parents."

"What parents?" Remo asked.

"Well, that damned little girl. I had a demonstration of teaching to swim through imagination. Little bitch."

"What happened?" said Remo.

"Panicked. Didn't trust me. I told her if she panicked, she'd drown, but if she relaxed, she'd be fine. Had the parents' signature on the release form too. But you know the courts in America. Didn't let it hold up. It would have been a breakthrough. Could have sold the program by mail order if it had worked."

"You took the life of a child?" said Chiun.

"She took her own life. If she had listened to me, she would have swum right out. I would have been famous. But the little bitch called out for her mommy. Damn. Had the local press there too."

"I see," said Chiun. "If the child had followed your instructions, she would have lived."

"Absolutely. One hundred percent. Lord's honest truth," said Charlese.

20

"Then I will show you how to walk walls," said Chiun, "for no secrets should be kept from one of such great faith."

This surprised Remo, because he knew that for the most deadly killers the world had ever known, the purposeful killing of a child was anathema. And there could be no question that Charlese's accident was not purposeful killing. Not to a master of Sinanju, Remo knew, because while discipline for adults was screw-lock tight, children were considered incapable of anything but receiving love. You nourished a child with love for the long hard journey through a life that had so little love.

This teaching, Chiun said, would occur at night. Remo listened to him talk. Some of what he said to Dr. Charlese was Sinanju, but most was, as Chiun often said, chicken droppings.

Early evening there was a phone call. Remo's Aunt Mildred was going to the country. She would be there at 3 A.M., and Remo should not worry about her kidney stones. It was a telegram read by Western Union. Remo did not worry about his Aunt Mildred or her kidney stones. He had no Aunt Mildred. He had no living relatives, which was precisely why he had been chosen more than a decade before by the people who hired Chiun to train him.

At 1 A.M., with Dr. Charlese bubbling over with speculation on the potential of the human mind, Chiun, Remo and Charlese walked fifteen flights up a back stairway to the roof. Below them Mexico City, once a city built on a swamp and now a modern city built on the rubble of ancient cities, twinkled brightly. The air was dusty hot, even at night, and the roof above the playroof gave no relief. The air covered them like a pressure cooker lid. Charlese's fancy clothes were darkened with perspiration. The front of his shirt looked as if someone had thrown a bucket of water at his navel.

"Do you believe?" asked Chiun.

"I believe," said Dr. Charlese.

"Do your breathing thing and then I shall show you a miracle," said Chiun.

Charlese closed his eyes and breathed deeply three times.

"I'm ready," he said.

"Your body is air," Chiun said softly in a dull monotone. "You float like a balloon. You are on a path. Solid. Walk. You feel a little wall in the middle of the path."

Charlese touched the small rail separating him from the sidewalks of Mexico City, one foot forward, thirty stories down.

"Climb over the small wall and rest your feet on the step beneath it. They are wide steps but you will use only a small part of them. You are secure. You are on wide steps. You are safe," said Chiun.

Charlese lowered his feet over the wall while the trunk of his body rested on the ledge.

"Yep, I feel the steps," said Charlese. "Hot dayum. It's working!"

Remo knew that what Charlese felt were the crevices between bricks. People could use the tips of the bricks for short climbing, but most people lacked the balance for anything more than a momentary step.

22

"You walk safely down the steps, the broad steps," said Chiun. Charlese's body went down, a brick's height at a time. Remo joined Chiun at the edge of the roof. Charlese went down the side of the building slowly, supported by his heels which lodged in the thin mortar cracks between bricks. The top of his body was visible. Then his shoulders. Then only his head.

"You can turn around on this wide step," said Chiun, and Charlese slowly turned his body so he was facing the wall. His smile looked to Remo like a crease in a fat melon. His eyes were closed.

"Open your eyes," said Chiun.

"It's working. It's working. I'll be rich," said Charlese, looking up at Remo and Chiun.

"Now," said Chiun, holding forth a finger, "I give you a most important piece of advice. Like you gave the child in the pool."

"I know, I know," said Charlese. "I won't muck it up."

"The advice is this: Do not think of what your body will look like when it falls that great distance to the ground," said Chiun.

The face went. Thwit. First it was smiling at them, and then it was gone. The hands, clutching desperately for a hold on something, anything, followed like two half-ounce bobbers yanked by a whale on the dive. Gone.

"I told him not to think what his body would look like when it reached the ground. I hope he listened to me," said Chiun.

Down below, a long way away, there was a distant clap, like a blob of fresh pizza dough smacking a cold tile. It was Charlese.

"I think the kitchen is closed by now. I'd like some fish, if you can get it without butter on it," Remo said.

"It is always a risk when someone else prepares your food," said Chiun. "You put their hands in your stomach. That is the risk.

"Smitty sent word earlier. There's some trouble. He'll be here in a couple of hours."

Remo opened the roof door for the Master of Sinanju. They descended the fifteen flights to their suite.

"Trouble? Emperor Smith faces trouble? Good. An emperor is always more reasonable when he is in trouble. The calm waters are starvation time for an assassin. For then he is cheated and reviled and disrespected. At times like these, we must compensate for those placid times."

"You're not going to hit him for another raise?" asked Remo.

"It is not a raise like some sweeper of dirt or planter of seed, but just an honest tribute to the House of Sinanju."

"Sure, sure," mumbled Remo. He knew gold was delivered by submarine to this village in North Korea, as stipulated in the agreement between Dr. Harold W. Smith, representing his organization, and Chiun, representing the village. This amount of gold—Chiun did not accept paper money considering it only a promise dependent upon the veracity of the sponsoring government—had steadily increased over the decade, the biggest jump coming most recently, when Chiun had insisted that the amount be doubled because Remo could now be considered a Master of Sinanju also, since he would one day succeed Chiun, and therefore the village deserved double compensation for double masters.

Remo shut the door of the suite behind them.

"Our tribute must be doubled again because . . ." said Chiun.

"Because why, Little Father?"

"I am thinking."

"You'll find something."

"I detect anger in your voice."

"I don't think it's fair to Smitty."

"Fair?" said Chiun, his longer fingernails fluttering before him, shock upon his normally placid face. "Fair? Was it fair when Tamerlaine all but closed the East for productive work, during the reign of his descendants? Was it fair during the gruesome depths of European history?"

The gruesome depths Chiun referred to was the condition of Europe after Napoleon, when there was almost a century of peace interrupted by only one short war. And worse, there were no pretenders to thrones intriguing to unseat one king or another with the silent hand during the night. During those years, the rations were meager in the village of Sinanju.

"It may come as a shock to you, Little Father, but Smitty is not the Austro-Hungarian empire."

"He is white. I am only making up for what other whites have done to the House of Sinanju. How they have cheated the House of Sinanju."

"Nobody lives to cheat the House of Sinanju."

"There is cheating and there is cheating. If I pay you less than you are worth, which seems im-

25

possible, then I am cheating you. If I do this just because you are willing to take less, then I am still cheating you."

"When did this happen?"

"According to your calendar, 82 B.C., 147 A.D., 381 A.D., 562 A.D., 904 A.D., 1351 A.D., 1822 A.D., and 1944 A.D., the Depression."

"The Depression? There was a world war going on then."

"For the House of Sinanju that is a Depression. Everybody hires local talent."

"That's the draft," said Remo.

And Chiun explained that for the House of Sinanju, the good times were when there were small wars and rumors of wars, when societies verged on revolution and when leaders slept uneasily because of nagging thoughts of who might depose them. These were such times and as the Master of Sinanju, it behooved Chiun to bargain effectively, for—as it always happened periodically—either a very fierce war using amateur help or a deep and severe peace using no one was right around the corner.

"I wouldn't mind peace, Little Father, and each man dwelling in his home without fear of his neighbor. I believe in those things. That's why I work for Smitty."

"That is all right, Remo. I am not worried. You will grow up. After all, you have only been learning for a few short years now."

And once again Chiun repeated the tale of Sinanju, how the village was so poor that for lack of food the newborn were not allowed to live and mothers had put their babies into the cold waters of the bay, until Sinanju sent out its masters to save the lives of the children.

"Think of that when you want peace," said Chiun righteously.

"That hasn't happened for more than two thousand years, Little Father," said Remo.

"Because we did not think like you," said Chiun, equating Remo's desire for peace with murdering the babies of Sinanju. Chiun would no longer discuss this with someone who had been given the secrets of Sinanju, a white no less, and then had turned his back on the cries of little children.

At 3 A.M. precisely, Dr. Harold W. Smith arrived, gaunt, grim-faced, with a lemony purse to his lips. In a collage of gaudy tourist fashion, his gray suit and vest and striped Dartmouth tie stood out like a tombstone at a birthday party.

"Glad to see you're looking well, Smitty," said Remo, assuming that this was well, since he had never really seen Smith any other way. Once, seven years before, Remo thought he had seen Smitty smile. The thin lips had risen slightly on both sides, a barely perceptible altering of the facial muscles. Remo had smiled back until he had found out it was caused by a toothache. Smitty had put off seeing a dentist.

"Remo," said Smith by way of greeting. "And Chiun, Master of Sinanju."

Chiun did not answer.

"Is something wrong?" Smith asked.

"No," said Remo. "Business as usual."

Chiun turned. "Hail, Emperor Smith," he said. "Oh, glorious defender of the great document, the

27

holy Constitution, wise and benificent ruler of the organization. The Master of Sinanju regrets not observing you properly at the outset, but my heart is troubled and my soul is deeply rent for the problems that beset your poor servant."

"We already increased the gold allotment to Sinanju," Smith said.

"Quite so," said Chiun, bowing. Remo was not surprised to see him accept this rebuff so cordially and easily. He knew Chiun had merely shifted his approach, not his purpose.

"We'll have to talk here," said Smith. "We can't use the roof, which is usually safest. Police are all around. Somebody jumped to his death or was pushed."

"Yeah," said Remo, looking at Chiun.

"How horrible," Chiun said. "Life becomes more dangerous every day."

Smith nodded curtly and continued. The problem was so grave that if they did not solve it, all the work of the organization since its inception might as well not have happened at all. Smith spoke for ten minutes, avoiding specifics in case there was a bug in the room.

From what Smith had said, Remo surmised there was now a system under which witnesses could be protected. With this system, prosecutors around the nation had begun to make significant inroads into the organized crime structure. It was the most successful program so far of the organization, and within five years could cause the syndicates to crumble because they could not hold the loyalty of their members without assuring them reasonable safety from jail. With this system, the top men in these crime structures were no longer safe. An aide could be promised immunity and a new life for testifying. The code of silence, *omerta*, was being broken daily.

That was, until recently. Somehow someone had found a way to get to the witnesses. Three in one day.

"Hmmmm," said Remo, seeing more than a decade of work trickle away. The purpose of the organization was, quite simply, to make the constitution work. The very safeguards that protected the citizen also made it possible for well-financed destructive elements to become virtually unprosecutable. Had this continued, the nation would have had to abandon the Constitution and become a police state. So, many years before, a now-dead President set up a small group headed by Dr. Harold W. Smith. Its budgets were siphoned from other agencies, its employees did not know for whom they worked, and only Smith and each succeeding president would know it existed. For to admit that the government was breaking the law in order to enforce it, was to admit that the Constitution did not work.

Therefore, the organization, CURE, did not exist—and when it needed an enforcement arm, they selected someone without living relatives, framed him for a murder he did not commit, secretly presided over his public "electrocution" (one of the last men to die in the chair in New Jersey), and made sure this electrocution didn't work quite properly, so that when Remo Williams awoke, he was publicly a dead man. A man who didn't exist for the organization which didn't exist.

They had done enough psyche tests to know this man would serve. On that first day after his visit to the electric chair, he had met Chiun and started the long journey along the road no white man had ever walked before, that only those from the village of Sinanju had ever trod.

Now he' was two men: the man who would serve CURE and the younger Master of Sinanju. And the man who would serve heard how more than a decade of work was disappearing, while the younger Master of Sinanju cared only about approaching that ultimate use of the human body and mind called Sinanju.

And both of them saw Chiun nod wisely and tell Dr. Harold W. Smith that Chiun commiserated with the emperor's problems—to a Master of Sinanju, a president, chairman, czar, king, dictator, director ... were all emperors—but it would be impossible to continue service to Emperor Smith. The House of Sinanju was withdrawing from the organization. This time for good.

"But why?" said Dr. Smith.

"Because this time we do not dispose of your enemies but suffer our own demise. It is written." Chiun was somber. His eyes lowered. "We are through."

Smith asked if it were more gold the House of Sinanju wanted, but Chiun responded there were some things that could not be purchased for gold.

"I'll double the tribute to the village," said Smith. And then, hesitantly, "if that will do any good."

"You cannot purchase our services for mere gold," said Chiun, "because you have already pur-

30

chased our undying loyalty with your awesome grace, oh, Emperor Smith."

And, added the Master of Sinanju, the doubling of the tribute to Sinanju exhibited the very essence of that grace.

CHAPTER THREE

Martin Kaufmann was screaming at the post commander when Chiun and Remo arrived at Fort Bragg, North Carolina. As Kaufmann shrieked it, he was not a member of the Airborne, had not been in the service for twenty-three years, was not under arrest and therefore, as an American citizen, he had a complete and legal right to leave. Just walk out, if you please.

As Major General William Tassidy Haupt responded, without even the movement of a finger on his clear and immaculate desk top:

"Personnel assigned under jurisdiction of the Department of Justice shall not exercise freedom of movement beyond post confines and within these said confines shall, at the discretion of the post commander, be restricted to areas deemed safe, beneficial and in accordance with the proper function of the unit's mission, heretofore determined by Regulations 847-9 and 111-B, paragraph 2-L of the latter."

And as Remo who had presented his credentials just moments before to Major General William Tassidy Haupt said:

"What're you dingies talking about?"

"I'm a prisoner," yelled Kaufmann, small blue veins popping around his light blue eyes. He was in his late fifties and had an accountant's gentle paunch under his blue and gold Bermuda shirt. He wore white sandals and white tennis shorts.

"He is a special guest who has signed Form 8129-V, granting and deeming certain prerogatives to the post commander as to area of abode and movement therein," said General Haupt. He too was in his late fifties but his body was trim, his eyes clear, his jaw set, his hair combed immaculately, as if each strand was organized and filed above his head. He looked as if he were waiting for a magazine photographer who wanted a model of a modern major general for a bad article on "Meet Your Post Commander."

"Therein is the key word," said General Haupt. "Therein."

"I want to leave," yelled Kaufmann.

"Did you or did you not sign Form 8129-V of your own free will?" said General Haupt.

"I signed a load of papers. I guess I signed that one."

"Then there is nothing to argue about," said General Haupt. "These men from the Justice Department will tell you that."

"I ordinarily do not interfere in white affairs," said Chiun.

"Executive order 1029-V, there shall be no

function assigned to race or religion. Go ahead, sir," said General Haupt to Chiun.

"This man who is afraid lacks confidence in your defenses and therefore seeks others."

"You're damned right. I'm scared shitless," said Kaufmann. "They're gonna get me."

General Haupt thought about this a moment. His face puzzled into little furrows above his eyes.

"Defenses?" he asked.

"Protection," said Chiun. "Those who fear attack have defenses."

"Like in wars and things," said General Haupt. "That's old stuff. Haven't dealt with that since the Point. An attack is like an assault, right?"

Chiun nodded.

"Yeah, I know what it is now," said General Haupt. "They happen during wars and things."

"If this man can be made to feel your defenses are safe, then there won't be any problem," said Remo.

"Good," said General Haupt. "That's not my mission. Outside my office you'll find a warrant officer. He will assign you to an official familiar with your specified function."

"Specified function?" said Remo.

"War and things. This is a modern army. We have people who are specialists for almost every function, no matter how exotic," said General Haupt.

"I don't care," said Kaufmann leaving the office with Remo and Chiun. "They're going to get me. I only said I'd testify because I was told, I was assured, I would be safe." And Kaufmann blurted out his story. He was a CPA who organized the books for a crime family in Detroit. His job was

34

surfacing money, that is, taking the huge excess amounts of illegal cash from gambling, narcotics, prostitution, and making it public in housing developments, banks, and shopping centers.

Remo nodded. All the money in the world was worthless if you couldn't spend it. And to spend money in America you had to show where you got it. You couldn't say you were unemployed and buy a $125,000 house and two $20,000 automobiles. So the mobs consistently surfaced money through a web of banks and businesses and phony investors.

If Kaufmann were the man in charge of this, he was a hell of a find for a witness. His testimony alone could take apart the whole structure of an entire city. No wonder Smitty had called him a "high probable" target. It was Remo's job not so much to stop a hit, which he would do, but to find out from the hit man who had sent him, and then to find out from who sent him who had paid the sender, and keep moving back until he was at the nub of this thing, where he would eliminate it.

In the process, he was to find out how these people worked.

They had killed three already, two current and one past witness in Detroit operations. According to Smitty, not only the identities of these witnesses were supposed to be secret but their whereabouts were supposed to be unknown outside the Justice Department. One by a bomb and two by gunshots. No one was seen around the schoolyard or the other two death scenes, who had not been, in Justice Department parlance, totally "clean."

The two gun deaths had been done with .22

caliber bullets, so long-distance sniping was out. Someone had gotten close without being seen. The Justice Department, and ultimately CURE, did not know who or how. Remo estimated Kaufmann's chances of survival as fifty-fifty—at best.

Feeling very governmental, Remo looked Kaufmann in the eye. "You've got nothing to worry about," he said, putting a reassuring arm around Kaufmann's shoulder.

"Then what about that bombing in the Oklahoma schoolyard? The papers said that guy was named Calder. But I knew him as a bookkeeper. I knew he was talking. He was safe too."

"That was an entirely different situation," lied Remo. He and Chiun walked along pin-neat paths of Fort Bragg, where white-painted stones like piping marked where people should and should not walk. Large, fresh-painted signs pointed arrows toward jumbles of numbers and letters such as "Comsecpac 918-V."

It was as if 20,000 persons had descended on the piny woods of North Carolina for the sole purpose of keeping this area neat—from time to time running around shooting off guns whose shell casings were collected, stacked, bound according to regulations, then shipped out to the Atlantic to be dumped by other men who kept ships just as neat.

A squad of men, rifles at port, jogged by in formation, chanting: "Airborne. Airborne." As Chiun had said of armies: "They are trained to smother their senses in order to perform duties, while Sinanju enhances the senses to perform more fully."

36

"How is it different for me and that poor bastard who got blown up?" asked Kaufmann.

"Look around you," said Remo. "Men with guns. Guards at gates. You're in the center of an organized fist, and it's protecting only you."

And Chiun nodded, saying something in Korean.

"What'd he say?" Kaufmann asked.

"He said you are probably the safest man in the world," said Remo, knowing that Chiun had noted that almost any attack could be foiled, except the one you were ignorant of.

"Who is he anyway?"

"A friend."

"How do I know you're not the killer? The mob had to get into the Justice Department somehow to even find that poor bastard in Oklahoma."

"Look, no weapons," Remo said, raising his arms.

"I still don't like it. You know what Polastro must be thinking since I left his payroll?"

"Polastro?" said Remo.

"Salvatore Polastro," said Kaufmann, slapping his forehead. "Oh, this is great. You're supposed to be special protection to me and you don't know who I'm testifying against."

"Good point," said Chiun.

"Thanks," said Remo and once more reassured Kaufmann. The lieutenant in charge pointed out that only families, trusted families, were allowed into what was now called Compound Seven.

Compound Seven had a gate, electronically wired. Compound Seven had constant security with ten-minute two-man patrols round the clock. Compound Seven had total control over entrance

37

and egress. Everyone had to have a pass or to be recognized. Compound Seven had metal security detection, thereby identifying every piece of metal anyone tried to carry into the compound.

"Most secure area outside of a SAC base, sir," the lieutenant told Remo.

"A death trap," Chiun said in Korean.

"What'd he say, what'd he say?" Kaufmann asked.

"He said the most secure area outside of a SAC base," Remo said.

"No, him," said Kaufmann, pointing to Chiun.

"He just commented on the compound. Relax, you have nothing to fear but fear itself."

Chiun cackled and said to Remo in Korean: "What silliness. Would you say that the only trouble with seeing danger is your eyesight? Would you say that the only trouble with hearing a great animal approach you was your ears? Why do you indulge in this silliness? Fear, like any other sense, helps prepare you for danger."

"You don't understand governments, Little Father."

"No, it is that I *do* understand governments."

"What're you two talking about?" said Kaufmann. "I'm surrounded by beanbags, and I'm going to die."

"General Haupt is the safest post commander in the Armed Forces," said the lieutenant.

"That's like hearing an unbiased endorsement of the Pope from an archbishop," Kaufmann said. "I'm leaving."

Remo followed him to his neat frame house surrounded by the same white-painted rocks that seemed to mark everything at the base. Two MPs, one with .45 caliber pistol at the ready, demanded Remo's identification before they let him follow Kaufmann inside. Another MP sat in the living room. He too demanded the same identification. Upstairs, Kaufmann was throwing clothes into a valise.

"Don't come near me. One yell and those MPs will be all over the place."

"And you want to leave this kind of security?"

"Yep."

"Why?"

"Because if they got that guy in Oklahoma, they're gonna get me."

"Where are you going to run to?"

"Not telling anyone."

"Is there no way I can convince you to stay?"

"No way," said Kaufmann, shoving a shirt and a handful of socks into the valise and compressing the jumble with the valise lid. *Snap.* "No way."

"The government needs you as a witness. Why don't you listen to my point of view?"

"You've got three seconds," said Kaufmann.

In that three seconds, Remo rose to his pinnacle of excellence. He explained how society depended upon citizens caring about justice. He said that when destructive elements such as Polastro were put to rout, the more constructive elements could flourish. He explained the responsibility of a citizen in a free society.

He also pressed an upper vertebra full into the cranial socket so that Kaufmann at first feared he would die as lights danced before his darkening eyes and then wished he would as every socket in his body felt as though it had been brushed with Number Two sandpaper.

39

Remo rested Kaufmann softly on the bed by the valise.

"Ohhh," said Kaufmann, waiting for the pain to subside so he could cry in agony.

"So you see how you fit into the plans of better government," said Remo.

Kaufmann saw that indeed. He assented by nodding his head. The nod was very sincere. So much did Kaufmann wish to show civic consciousness that he touched his head to his knees and rolled to the floor. A deep nod.

"On behalf of the government of the United States and the American people, I thank you," Remo said.

Downstairs, Remo smiled to the living room MP. He heard a shriek from upstairs. It was Kaufmann getting back his lungs. The pain was, of course, momentary. Chiun called the pressure move "the fallen petal" and said it worked because of a disruption of life forces and death forces which coexisted in the human body. Remo had tried to discover what it meant in Western terms, and the closest he could figure out was that it was a forced disfunction of the nervous system. Except that according to the medical books the recipient of that sort of pressure should die. They never did.

The MP ran upstairs. Outside, the door two guards stopped Remo until it was fully determined that said disturbance was not related in any manner, physical or otherwise, to current temporary personnel.

"Which means what?"

"Which means you don't move till we find out

what happened upstairs," said the MP with the unholstered .45.

The living room guard stuck his head out of an upstairs window.

"He says it's all right," the MP called. "He just keeps repeating how he supports constructive elements."

Chiun watched this and commented:

"The fallen petal."

Three young boys, one with a plastic baseball bat, ran into the yard and pushed their way past Remo. Did Mr. Kaufmann want to play pitch? one of them yelled. "No," came Kaufmann's voice from upstairs—but they could have some cookies if they wished.

"Sorry we had to detain you," said the MP to Remo, with an official smile that showed neither regret nor remorse. One of the boys threw a white plastic ball at his head and it bounced off.

On the neat grass-ordered street of the compound, with the smells of dinner coming from the homes and with the sun hot over the Carolinas, Remo asked Chiun why he called the compound a death trap.

"I figured fifty-fifty myself," Remo said.

"Those are odds of probability, correct?"

"Yeah," said Remo.

"Then ninety-fifty against," said Chiun.

"It's got to come out a hundred."

"Then a hundred against."

"A certainty?" Remo asked.

"Almost a certainty."

"Well, that's ninety-nine to one."

"Granted," said Chiun. "Ninety-nine to your

41

one that this Mr. Kaufmann is a dead man. His instinct to run was correct."

"How can you say that?"

"Do you know how the other safe ones were killed?"

"No, which is why I figure these safety measures make it fifty-fifty."

"If you have a bowl of rice, and if this bowl of rice is on the ground, and if someone steals the rice?"

"Yeah?" said Remo.

"What would you do?"

"I'd protect the rice."

"Ah, good. How?"

"Put a watchdog on it."

"And if the next day, the watchdog were killed?"

"Build a fence around it."

"And if the next day the rice was gone and the fence still there?"

"Camouflage the rice. I now have a fucking camouflaged bowl of rice with a leaky fence and a dead dog."

"And on the morrow that rice is gone also, what would you do?"

"Think of something else, obviously."

"And just as obviously that something else would fail."

"Not necessarily," said Remo.

"Yes, necessarily," said Chiun.

"How can you say that?"

"It is simple," said Chiun. "You cannot defend against what you do not know."

"Maybe that other thing would work. I know it's not the best odds, but it's not a certainty."

"Yes, a certainty," said Chiun. "There is no such thing as luck. Only beneficial things which people do not understand. That is the only luck."

"Then what about my good fortune in learning Sinanju?"

"A very simple answer," said Chiun, and Remo was sorry he had even mentioned this, for he knew what was coming, was certain of it when he saw the contented smile grace the delicate parched features of the Master of Sinanju.

"My decision to teach you, to make you Sinanju, can be explained simply," said Chiun. "Since a little child, I have always attempted to exceed these laws. Like attempting to transform a pale piece of a pig's ear into something worthy or making diamonds out of mud. You have heard it. I have admitted flaw. My choice of you."

"Well, then," said Remo, and his voice was a snarl, "you know, I've just about had enough of this crap. I'm as good as most previous masters except maybe you, and if you want to pack it in, then you know you can pack it in."

"Anger?" asked Chiun.

"Not anger. Go spit in a windstorm."

"Over a little jest, such hurt?"

"I'm a little bit tired of that dump you call a village in North Korea. I've seen it. If it were in America, they'd condemn the thing."

Chiun's smile descended.

"How typical to turn a little harmless jesting into vicious slander." And Chiun became silent and moved off to the other end of the compound. Remo waited by the fence. He tossed a whiffle ball with a few children, showing them how you could make it rise as well as drop, making it appear to

43

stay motionless in the hot summer evening air. One of the MPs tried to imitate the trick and couldn't, even though he had once pitched for Tidewater in the International League. About 3:42 P.M., Remo heard two sharp taps, like a hammer hitting a nail into porcelain. He told the MPs to check on Kaufmann.

"What for?"

"I heard something," Remo said.

"I didn't hear anything," said the MP.

"Check," said Remo, and the way he said it seemed to indicate rank on his shoulder. It was something the MP just knew was to be done, not because of any visible rank but because of the man doing the ordering.

The MP rushed. Remo walked, although he knew what he would find. The two light taps were not something hitting, but small explosions of air. And he could not tell the MP that when your body was awake you felt sounds as well as heard them.

The living room guard was defending the cookies from an eleven-year-old girl who said Mr. Kaufmann always let her take seven oreos, and the guard answering that even if Mr. Kaufmann did let her take seven, which he sincerely doubted, he knew her mother wouldn't let her take seven and put six back. Now.

He came out of the kitchen when he heard them, but Remo and the other MP were up the stairs to Kaufmann's bedroom before he could ask what was going on.

They found Kaufmann sitting on the floor, his legs stretched in front of him, his hands at his sides. His shoulders were pressed against a picture

44

that had been ripped from its hook above him on the wall. He had obviously leaned back against the picture, then slid to the floor, taking the picture with him. His eyes were closed. A reddish trickle worked its way down his flaming Bermuda shirt. The shoes jumped as though jolted by a small charge of electricity.

"Thank God he's alive," said the MP. "Must have fallen and cut himself."

"He's dead," said Remo.

"I just saw him move."

"That's just the body getting rid of the last energy it won't need anymore. It's the life force leaving."

Kaufmann, it was later determined, was killed by two .22 caliber bullets that entered under the chin and lodged in the brain. The special personnel from the Justice Department, the caucasian called Remo and his Oriental colleague, were, as General Haupt put it in his report, unaccounted-for unindigenous personnel of now-questionable credentials.

It was in this heat of battle that Major General William Tassidy Haupt, showed how he had earned his stars and why his men had always called him "the safest damned general in the whole damned Army."

First, under the heavy artillery of Washington pressure, he set his emergency flanking moves. He immediately established a top-secret investigating commission with a young colonel at its head. This commission was to see where the lieutenant had failed. Like other great commanders, General Haupt had taken proper precautions before the action. Cunningly, he had gotten an MP

45

detachment from Fort Dix, and in a daring move had stolen a march on the Fort Dix commander. The detachment from Fort Dix was the very detachment that was assigned to guard Kaufmann. Of this, General Haupt had said nothing, letting the MPs' orders come from the New Jersey post, secret and confidential to the lieutenant leading the detachment. Haupt's chief of staff did not at first understand this, but later, on the day Kaufmann was killed, this mysterious little bit of paperwork showed itself to be Haupt's true genius. For when Kaufmann was killed, Haupt moved with precision under fire. It was his colonel investigating the Fort Dix failure. Not only was Fort Bragg not charged with failure, it became the outfit that would assign blame.

He also showed flexibility, even while the attorney general was on the phone, a full cabinet member, coming on with everything he had. General Haupt launched his main attack, right into the teeth of official Washington.

"The last people seen with the subject, Kaufmann, were accredited by your department, Mr. Attorney General. I have the forms right here."

"What are you saying?"

"Perhaps Fort Dix was at fault. We don't know yet. I'm not going to hang a fellow Army officer when it appears that the Justice Department itself might have been responsible for Kaufmann's mishap. The caucasian and the Oriental, who are now prime suspects, were your people."

Haupt's chief of staff gasped. A captain, who had just come from the Pentagon where one did not frontally assault any other agency, let alone a full cabinet member, lost the strength of his legs and had to be helped from the room. A staff sergeant stared dumbly ahead. No one saw his knuckles whitening.

Haupt held the phone without amplifying his statement, letting it run full and strong. The line to Washington was quiet. Haupt covered the mouthpiece of the phone.

"He's checking it out," said Haupt and winked at the captain. It was good to show the troops a bit of levity under fire. It quieted them down and steeled their nerves.

"I think you're right," said the attorney general. "It wasn't normal channels but those two did have Justice Department clearance. We're checking it out now." Haupt had put the telephone on loudspeaker so his staff could listen in.

"I want to assure you, sir," said Haupt, "that you will get a fair and impartial investigation." And he hung up.

Haupt's chief of staff, an old campaigner who had done ten uninterrupted years in the middle of official Washington, was the first to realize what had happened. Fort Bragg had the Justice Department itself on the run and should Justice somehow be able to turn this brilliant attack around, it could only hit Fort Dix. It was all systems go and ride to glory. A disaster turned into a victory.

He jumped up and with a shout gave his commanding officer a booming slap on the back.

"You tough old bastard, you did it again," he shouted. The captain, too, suddenly realized they had won.

"Wow," he said with a great gush of air. "I

wouldn't have believed it if I hadn't seen it." The staff sergeant, his chest glistening with ribbons won in offices from Weisbaden to Tokyo, just grinned.

"If I may say so, sir, you've got balls."

General Haupt accepted the adulation, then suddenly became somber.

"Let's not forget that the Justice Department has human beings too. The poor devils."

"What about the Fort Dix commander?" asked the captain.

"I'll try to get him out if I can," said General Haupt. "But he had no business in this game. It's what happens when you have unprepared green, raw personnel. He was always in over his head."

"But the Fort Dix commander is a general too, sir," said the captain.

"I think the colonel can better explain," said General Haupt.

"Thank you, sir," said the colonel and rose to speak.

"Yes, the general at Fort Dix would appear to be a general. But only by an act of Congress and official promotions. You see, he has spent an entire career outside of the main action. No real Army experience."

"I don't understand," said the captain.

"You take a man out of West Point," said the colonel, "and you put him directly in charge of a combat platoon in France during World War II. You keep him on maneuvers until the Korean War and then let him do nothing but command a battalion against the Chinese Reds and the North Koreans and before he gets any real experience, you put him into Vietnam in charge of a combat division. Where the hell is he ever going to get real experience? The man doesn't know how to make a speech or how to talk to a foreign diplomat or a visiting congressman."

"I see," said the captain.

"It's tough, but it's life," said General Haupt. "If you want to go shooting Horlands at someone, join the National Rifle Association or the Mafia. But stay the hell out of this man's Army."

"Howitzers, sir. They're not called Horlands."

"When you've served as many years in this man's Army as I have," said Major General William Tassidy Haupt, "you don't have time to indulge yourself in that kind of thing. If they had had real generals in charge, we never would have gotten into Vietnam. Any shavetail could have seen there were no votes there, no industrial power there, absolutely no political sock. But you take that childish mentality that always wanted to play soldier and they think you can solve all your basic problems by shooting Horlands at them."

"Howitzers at them, sir."

"Whatever," said General Haupt. "Let's get a drink. It's been a long day."

In Folcroft Sanitarium on Long Island Sound, Smith read the multitude of reports. Since the outset, he had carefully managed to jump the lines of official Washington so that what one office of official Washington thought would be seen only by another office, also went to this sanitarium. The increasing use of computers simplified this. You didn't need a person to feed you a secret re-

49

port. You merely plugged in, and Folcroft had one of the largest computer banks in the world.

Smith pondered the latest reports. Four witnesses dead. No one seen entering the premises. The waves became dark and gloomy over the sound. A storm threatened. A small Hobie Craft, its sail full-gusted from the growing northeaster, skimmed its way into port.

The witness system was a foundation of everything the organization had worked for these many years. If that worked, organized crime would be through. Of course, there was the growing inability of police to cope with street crime and that too could cause a disenchantment so deep as to bring in a police state. But that was something else, a second problem to solve. And when both those problems had been solved, Smith and CURE could close shop.

Right now, all the work done, all the blood spilled, seemed like so much waste matter on the landscape. Where witnesses did not feel safe to testify, there was no such thing as a working judicial system.

He had played his two top cards, and not only had they failed, but they had become suspects.

Smith fingered a report. It was an interdepartmental memo from a William Tassidy Haupt, Maj. Gen., USA. A skilled bureaucrat, Haupt had made Remo and Chiun with their "Justice Department" credentials the major suspects.

Haupt. Haupt? The name was familiar.

Of course. Smith punched a retrieve program from the terminal at his desk. In all Folcroft, this was the only terminal that could retrieve an entire program. Others could get only parts with words, letters, and numbers missing.

Haupt, Lt. Col, USA, killed in action, Bastogne, 1944. Right. Right. Smith had remembered the name for a very special reason. He had just been out of Dartmouth and beginning what he thought was an interim career for the government, during World War II, when someone had mentioned that this Colonel Haupt could not be relied on for combat. Colonel Haupt was a bureaucrat who had remained a captain from 1922 to 1941. He was unprepared for war, and what always happened to peacetime armies happened. The combat people took command from the peace people. Colonel Haupt was assigned to a supply battalion. He had been with it when everything was overrun in the Ardennes. Instead of surrendering when it appeared hopeless, Haupt destroyed the supplies rather than let them fall into enemy hands, and then turned his unit into a guerilla band working behind German lines.

Smith, with the OSS, had been assigned to find out if the Germans had enough petrol to make this last offensive stick, and parachuted in behind lines to meet Haupt's little band. Not only had Colonel Haupt prepared a correct analysis of the enemy's fuel supply but as if guided by some genius hand, had known it was the fuel that was the key, and had been attacking just that in his small assaults on the Nazis.

That cold Christmas Colonel Haupt fought with his intestines held inside him by tape. He literally fought while he was dying. There was nothing dramatic about it, and Colonel Haupt did not become one of the better-known heroes of the

51

Battle of the Bulge. One afternoon, the day before the skies cleared enough for Smith to be picked up, Lt. Col. William Haupt rested against the base of a tree and didn't get up.

A hell of a soldier.

He had a son. Haupt, William Tassidy, Maj. Gen., USA.

Maybe like father, like son.

Smith picked up one of the blue phones on his desk. It took longer to get Fort Bragg than a normal phone call would have. This was because the blue phone was a rerouter that switched Smith's calls through various trunk lines in the Midwest before completing them. If any of his calls were ever traced, the call would be terminated in Idaho or Ohio or Wisconsin and no one would ever be able to connect the harmless sanitarium on the Long Island Sound with the phone call.

A general's aide answered. Smith said it was the Pentagon calling and Haupt should answer immediately.

"He's busy now, sir, can he call you back? I didn't get your name."

"You will put General Haupt on this line within one minute or your career and his career are over," Smith said.

"Hello, General Haupt here."

"General Haupt, I have read your report on the Kaufmann killing and it does not look good."

"Who am I talking to?"

"I don't like your suspects."

"Who is this?"

"Someone who knows you've taken the nearest convenient suspects instead of risking looking for the real ones."

"I do not have to conduct a conversation with anyone who does not identify himself."

"Your career, General. It's through. You'll have the real killers or you'll be through." Smith glanced at the small file on the general. There was some small mention of a disorderly conduct incident while the general was at the Point. It occured in New Paltz, New York.

"We know about the New Paltz incident, General."

"Hah," boomed General Haupt. "I was found innocent. I was, I believe, nineteen years old at the time."

"But we know you were guilty," said Smith, taking a calculated shot in the dark. Courts in those days were reluctant to convict West Point cadets for minor offenses because the young men could be thrown out of the Academy for even such minor infractions.

"Who the hell is this?"

"The people who are going to end your career."

"This is rubbish. Besides, I can't be held responsible for failure by Fort Dix personnel."

"Your career, General."

"If you're CIA, you're in more trouble nowadays than I am. You're vulnerable."

"Your career," said Smith and with a dramatic dry little chuckle, Smith hung up.

Maybe, like father, like son. CURE needed something. It had played its two top cards and not only had the finest assassins in history failed to protect the witnesses but they had no idea how the killing was done. Sinanju, whose every master had carefully studied the methods of whatever country he was in, did not know how these witnesses were being killed. More than two thousand years of learning stymied.

Like father, like son. Hopefully. Perhaps Haupt could get a lead where Smith and his organization had failed.

CHAPTER FOUR

Salvatore Polastro, president of Dynamics Industries, Inc., Polastro Real Estate, Inc., CompSciences, Inc., and exalted grand leader of the Detroit Grand Council of Buffaloes—a civic and fraternal organization—had finished dedicating the new Holy Name sports complex and was washing his hands when someone blended his left wrist into a stunning colies fracture.

He knew it was a colies fracture because while skiing three years earlier, he had suffered a similar injury, that time jamming his left hand into an oncoming skier and glare ice. Five breaks in his wrist. This time, turning on the water faucet in the boys' room of the Holy Name sports complex.

He had only turned the faucet left and then the hand would not turn anymore and there was this incredible pain. He lowered himself to his knees the better to cradle his left arm with. He did not even feel the soapy floor water on his knees. On his knees, he smelled the sink soap quite clearly because his face rested against the cool wash-basin.

"*Yaaaah,*" he groaned.

"Hello there," came a voice from behind him. "My name is Remo, and you're going to talk to me."

"*Yaaaahh,*" said Salvatore Polastro again.

"I'd appreciate something more than groans. You've caused me a problem. You're going to uncause it. How did you kill Kaufmann? Who did it for you? Did you arrange it?"

"My wrist. I can't talk."

"I left you your throat so you could talk. Now if you're not going to use it for me, I'll take it with me."

Polastro had not seen what had shattered his wrist. He hobbled around on the soapy floor so he could see his questioner. He saw two knee caps, two empty hands, a light sports shirt and a rather bored face. Since there was no blood in his broken wrist, the man must have used some instrument that didn't break skin to draw blood. But the man's hands were empty.

How did he get in here, anyway? Where were Tony and Vito? He'd settle the matter with those dumbhead bodyguards shortly. They live off you, fat and sloppy, and the first lunatic that makes an attempt at you succeeds.

"Time's up," said the man.

"In Chicago at the board of education, there's a man. He provides the service."

"The killings are contracted out?"

56

"Special ones. It's expensive. I ain't admitting that I contracted anything out. And none of this will hold up in a court. This is no confession."

"I'm not in the court business. How does this man do it?"

"I don't know. That's why he's expensive."

"His name?"

"I don't know his name."

"How expensive?"

"A hundred thousand in advance. A hundred thousand when the job's done."

"And you tell me you give a hundred thousand down to someone whose name you don't know?"

"Yes," said Salvatore Polastro and he saw a hand move very slowly down to his good, cradling, wrist. Slowly, yet it was out and back, and now his right wrist had that searing shock, that instant of pain that let him know it was more than a sprain that would go right away. He slumped back on his heels which were now beneath him. His two hands, loosely connected to arms by two broken wrists, lay useless in his lap.

"You phone a special number in Chicago, and then they call back and tell you where to send the money and they get all the information on the hit," Polastro said.

"I just need someone."

"The first call goes to a Warner Pell. He's the assistant director of special advancement progress."

"What does that mean?"

"He tries to keep the niggers and the retards away from ruining the students."

"With force?"

"I don't know. I don't know what he does. He's just assistant director of special advancement progress. You never know what they do. None of my business. Hey, let me get to a doctor."

"You're a racist," said Remo.

"Who isn't?"

"Lots of people."

And then Polastro saw an old Oriental shuffle into the boys' room of the new Holy Name sports complex. An old man he was, with long fingernails and wisps of white hair circling his frail golden skull like delicate ribbons.

"I heard that," he said. "Any system that keeps whites and blacks away from the real students is a good one."

What was that old man doing here? Where were Tony and Vito? They were letting people through like they were going through turnstiles.

"I know you wouldn't lie to us. Warner Pell, you say."

And Salvatore Polastro, a leading Detroit citizen, was about to say yes when everything became dark. When he woke up, both his hands were aching and they were heavy with white plaster casts. He saw a white ceiling light above him and that he was covered with a light gray blanket and white sheets. He was in a bed. He saw a black plastic knob hanging down from a black wire. It was a call button. He was in a hospital.

"Shit," said Salvatore Polastro.

"Sir, are you awake?" asked a nurse who was reading a magazine.

"No. I always talk in a coma," said Polastro. "Where are my chauffeur and secretary? Tony," he called out. "Vito. Vito. Tony."

"Sir, you'd better rest."

"I want Tony and Vito."

"Sir, they're indisposed."

"What does that mean?"

"They can't come here right now."

"You tell them I say so. They'll come."

"I'm afraid not, sir."

"Did they run away?"

"Not exactly, sir. They were found in the trunk of a car near the Holy Name sports complex. Just after the sisters found you unconscious on the floor with your wrists broken."

"Found? How were they found? They were big men."

"In the front trunk of a Volkswagen suffering traumatic hemorrhaging and severe bodily fractures."

"Which means what?"

"Squashed to jelly, sir."

"I figured. Okay. Make a phone call."

"I'm not allowed to. You're supposed to be sedated."

"Don't give me that shit. There's a sawbuck in it for you."

"I'm not going to violate my sacred nurse's pledge for a ten-dollar bill."

"A hundred."

"Long distance or local?"

Polastro got his number and had to offer another yard for the nurse to leave the room. First she had to cradle the telephone between his right ear and shoulder.

"Look," said Polastro, "don't answer. I'm going to talk. At the end, ask questions if you want. This is an open line. Both my wrists are broken. I've lost two of my best men. There are two men after you. They must use some kind of weird killing machines. I gave them your name. I had to. They would have killed me. But you can stop them. One's a gook."

"We understand and hope to work with you toward a progressive solution."

"That's good, right?"

"There's no good or bad. Just situations towards which we must harness community energy. Good-bye."

Polastro called back the nurse. This time he wanted a local call. This time, she could stay. The call was brief.

He wanted four men right away. No, he didn't care if they had records. To hell with the public front. His ass was at stake.

"That's a thousand," said the nurse. "I didn't know you were in the Mafia."

"Where do you get words like that?" said Polastro.

"Oh, I know. Everyone knows. You've got millions."

"Don't be ridiculous."

"I want a thousand dollars or I talk to anyone who will listen."

"We don't work that way."

And when the four men entered the hospital room twenty minutes later, the nurse knew what Mr. Polastro was talking about. She saw the faces, the cold black eyes, the sort of faces that said "we break open heads for a living" and she really did not want that much money. Not at all. She was glad to help.

"Give her a hundred bucks," said Polastro, and a single one-hundred-dollar bill came off a roll of bills as fat as a sink drain.

As Polastro explained his problem to the men who helped him out of the hospital room, a man to each arm, he now faced hit men whose method he did not know. Therefore, they had to be ready for anything. Anything. Electronics, bullets, hands, knives, anything.

"They gotta do it with something," said one of the men, honored to be promoted to personal bodyguard. "They don't walk through walls or nothing, right?"

Everyone but Polastro said, "Right." Polastro said, "I hope not."

The top two floors of one of his office buildings were vacant, so just in case his home in Grosse Point had been staked out, he put himself up in those two floors. The elevators were rigged to be unable to open their doors at these floors. A round-the-clock guard was put on the stairways and the roof. The windows were curtained off so no one at a distance could get in a sniper shot. The food was stored and prepared right in the top floor. One of the henchmen had to taste half of whatever was made, then Polastro would keep that bowl near him for an hour to make sure no one else touched it. At the end of the hour, he asked the taster how he felt. If the answer was fine, Polastro ate. If there was any question, any slight dizziness, Polastro would pass up the bowl. No one could leave the floors.

All telephones were cut off so none of the men could make an outgoing phone call. The only phone working was Polastro's which he kept in his lap.

This procedure lasted exactly twenty-four hours and thirty-one minutes. At 12:45 P.M. the

61

following day, the guards were called down from the roof, the shades were opened on the windows and everyone left—with the body of Salvatore Polastro, beloved father of Maureen and Anna, husband of Consuelo, president of Dynamics Industries, Inc., Polastro Real Estate, Inc., CompSciences, Inc., and exalted grand leader of the Detroit Council of Buffaloes.

"He will be sorely missed," said the chairman of the Holy Name sports complex building fund.

"Suddenly, of complications at his home in Grosse Pointe," the obituary read. The complication was above his waist. The bodyguards had difficulty scraping his torso off the walls and windowshades. The casts on his wrists, however, remained intact, prompting a hospital spokesman to comment that the "complications" could have had nothing to do with the very simple medical procedure at the hospital.

Polastro's death had been ordained by Dr. Harold W. Smith, in the faint hope that it might discourage others from availing themselves of the new contract-killing service that Remo had told Smith about. The idea was that there was no point in killing a witness to stay out of jail when that guaranteed you that you would wind up a greasy smudge on your living-room wall. Smith did not think it would work, but neither had anything else. It was worth a try.

Meanwhile, Remo and Chiun had arrived in Chicago with only three of Chiun's normal complement of fourteen large steamer trunks. They were not supposed to stay long, but Chiun had noted that Remo's plans did not seem to be working all that well.

"You mean I'm failing?"

"No. Sometimes events are stronger than people. To change thought patterns and action patterns because of difficulties is folly. That is failure."

"I don't follow, Little Father," said Remo who had expected an unbroken string of *I-told-you-sos* after the loss of Kaufmann, for had not Chiun warned there was no chance of saving the man. "Didn't you criticize me on the Army post for doing the same thing over and over again? Remember? The rice and the leaky fence and the dead dog?"

"You never listen. I did not criticize you for that. I was explaining a fact to you, that that man was dead. But I did not say you should change. If a farmer plants rice for tens of years and then one year he has a bad harvest, should he stop planting rice?"

"He should find out why the crop failed," Remo said.

"That would be nice, but not necessary," said Chiun. "He should keep planting rice in the way that has worked so many times before."

"Wrong," said Remo. "It's necessary to find out what went bad."

"If you say so," said Chiun with unexpected mildness.

"And another thing," said Remo. "Why aren't you carping as much as you usually do?"

"Carp?" said Chiun. "Is that not the word for complaining? Is that not the word for ridiculing? Is that not the word for incessant demeaning chatter?"

"It is," said Remo, watching the beefy cab

63

driver load Chiun's trunks into the back of the cab and the cab trunk and on the cab roof. The Chicago air smelled so heavily of soot you could ladle it into bowls. One of the disadvantages of using more of your senses was that when you were alive in air like this, you would just as soon have them dormant. To breathe Chicago air was a meal.

"You say I carp?" Chiun said.

"Well, yes. Sometimes."

"I carp?"

"Yes."

"I carp!"

"Yes."

"I take a pale piece of a pig's ear, raise it above what it came from, give it powers and senses beyond any its family history has ever known, and I carp.

"I glorify it beyond its boundaries and it goes around giving away secrets to a charlatan who babbles about mind waves and breathing. I give it wisdom and it spurns it. I nurture and love it and it produces putrescence and complaints that I carp. I carp!"

"Did you say 'love,' Little Father?"

"Only as a form of lying white speech. After all, I am a carper. I carp."

Chiun asked the cab driver, who was now facing heavy traffic on the way into downtown Chicago, whether he heard any carping.

"Of the two, who would you say is the carper?" Chiun demanded. "Be honest now."

"The white guy," said the cab driver.

"How did you do that?" Remo asked, not having seen any currency pass between Chiun and the driver or Chiun leaning into one of the man's pressure points.

"I trust in the honesty of our good driver. All in the West is not foul or ungrateful or complaining . . . I carp, *heh, heh,*" cackled Chiun. "I carp."

There were a multitude of reasons why Chiun could not possibly carp. Remo heard every one of them in detail on the way to the board of education, the last one being it was not Chiun who had lost Kaufmann, not Chiun who had said fifty-seven different gambling odds, not Chiun who had wasted his time at that Army post. Why not Chiun? Because Chiun was not a carper.

"Look, Little Father, I'm a bit worried. Smitty said we should stay away from Chicago until he could find out more about that guy. Maybe I'm not doing the right thing."

And on this rare occasion, the Master of Sinanju yelled: "Who have I taught, you or your Smith? Who knows what is right, some seedling emperor, of which are there many each generation, or the skilled product of Sinanju? You are wonderful, fool, and you do not comprehend this yet."

"Wonderful, Little Father?"

"Do not listen to me. I carp," said Chiun. "But know you this. While you were at that Army outpost, doing what a mere emperor told you to do, you failed. Now you will succeed because you do what you know to do, what I have taught you to do. Sitting, even a stone is not safe. Rolling, it carries all before it. Go."

At this point, the cab driver who had been expecting a big tip under the reasonable assumption that a lie was worth more than the truth in the tipping market, did note that perhaps the Oriental did carp a bit. However, he did not dwell on this. He had more important and immediate things, like getting his ears out of the triangular vent window of the front seat. His nose was very close to the outside mirror and his ears pinched as he tried to pull his head back through. What he could not figure out was how his head got there. He had made the comment about carping and then was wondering how to get his ears past the metal trim, back into the cab. If he could squeeze his ears through, he could get the rest of his head back in and that would be wonderful. It was what he wanted now more than anything else in the world. He heard the Oriental tell the white guy to trust himself and then the Oriental stopped the deafening clatter for a moment and the cab driver said:

"I was sort of wondering if you could help me, sort of, get back in the cab."

"You would ask a carper for help?"

"You don't carp," said the driver. He felt a fast warmth around his ears and then his head was back inside and what was most amazing was that the window panel wasn't bent. Sir, no sir, the sir wasn't a carper at all, sir, and yes sir, it was really amazing how people would not listen to good advice these days, sir.

Chiun thought so too. Even transportation servants, when properly reasoned with, could come to correct solutions.

Inside the Chicago board of education, something was wrong. People moved quickly, some

66

barking sharp commands. Knots of worried faces exchanged questions with each other.

"What happened?" came a voice. Several answered.

"Warner Pell. At his desk."

"What?"

"Dead."

"No."

"Yes."

"Oh, my God. No."

And while this was going on, another:

"What happened?"

"Warner Pell."

"What?"

"Dead."

"No."

"Yes."

"Oh, my God. No."

Remo intruded upon a knot of people.

"You say Warner Pell is dead?" Remo asked.

"Yes," said a fleshy-faced woman with large rhinestone eyeglasses hanging by a cord over widening breasts that seemed to strain her twenty-pound test weight nylon bra, like large formless vestigial lumps that might, ten or twenty years before, have been used to feed babies.

"How?" asked Remo.

"Shot to death. Murdered."

"Where?"

"Down the hall. Murder in the board of education. This is becoming as bad as a classroom. My God, what next?"

"As bad as a classroom," said another.

Remo spotted two blue uniforms down the

other end of the hallway. He still had his Justice Department identification. He used it.

The two patrolmen nodded Remo into the office. He sensed something was wrong, not by any overt movement, but by a sudden disruption of their rhythms. Unless people were aware of it and purposely controlled it, a sudden realization of the mind was displayed in the body. With some people it was a roar, like a Cary Grant double-take. With others, it was a more subtle deadening of the facial muscles. One cop had it, turned his back to Remo and whispered to the other who, of course, did not turn around to look at Remo, but if you watched his shoulders, they jerked upward as his mind responded.

A big cardboard sign hung outside the door to the inner office. It read:

Special Advancement Progress,
Warner Pell, Assistant Director
for Coordination

Inside, Pell was not coordinating anything. One arm rested on the side of a couch, the head was tilted back over a chest bib of blood. Someone had shot him several times under the chin. The dead eyes were directed at the ceiling. A police photographer clicked off a flash. Pell sat facing an undersized chair.

Remo showed his credentials.

"Know who did it?"

A detective whose white shirt had surrendered to the summer heat outside and whose face had made a similar pact with his job years before, said:

"No."

68

"How was it done?"

"A .25 caliber up through the chin."

"Then the killer had to be below him?"

"That's right," said the detective.

Again, a hit from below. That was how Kaufmann had gotten it also.

"Anybody see the killer leave?"

"No. Pell was interviewing some problem kid. Kid was in such a state of shock, he couldn't talk."

"Maybe the kid. How old is he?"

"A kid. Nine years old, for Christ's sake. You guys from Justice are real screamers. A nine-year-old kid, not a suspect."

"I thought he might have been fifteen or sixteen."

"Nah. A kid."

In the outer office, a white woman with a fierce Afro and an indignant scowl that could putrefy a mountain breeze, demanded to know what the police officers were doing disrupting her schedule. If the clothes had not flaunted such severe dark lines, with a heavy wide belt and a brass buckle that looked as it if shielded a foreign embassy instead of a navel, she might have been attractive. She was in her early thirties, but her mouth was in its fifties. She had a voice like boiling Drano.

A nine-year-old boy stood meekly at her side, looking for directions.

"I am Ms. Kaufperson and I demand to know what you police are doing here without my permission."

"There's been a homicide, lady."

"I am not your lady. I am a woman. You," she said to Remo. "Who are you? I don't know you."

69

"I don't know you, either," Remo said.

"I am the coordinating director of motivational advancement," she said.

"That's the retards," said one detective.

"No," said another. "Pell was the retards."

"What's motivational advancement?" Remo asked, watching the two patrolmen from outside close in on the door. Their guns were out. All right, two at one door, he'd go through them when they crossed, making sure they didn't fire their guns and hurt somebody in the room, especially the little boy who was with Ms. Kaufperson.

"Motivational advancement is exactly what it means. Through viable meaningful involvement we positively affect underachievers toward fuller utilization of their potential."

"That's lazy kids," said one detective.

Then the first patrolman at the door made his move. Stepping between Ms. Kaufperson and Remo, he pointed his revolver toward Remo, announcing: "Hold it, you. It's the suspect posing as Justice Department, Sergeant. He's the one. With that funny first name."

It was really a juggling act more than anything else. Remo had to keep the gun at him and the one drawn by the other patrolman and the two guns being drawn by the detectives from firing at anyone, preferably himself. So as the first announced that Remo should not move, he eased behind one detective and pushed him inside the angle of the gun arm of the patrolman and spun the second detective off into the corner and then simply moved himself through the falling bodies toward the last patrolman whose gun was up and

70

ready to fire. Remo put an index finger into the nerves of the gun hand. To an outsider it looked like a bunch of people-suddenly collapsing into each other while one rather thin man seemed to walk through them quietly.

None of the moves were particularly exotic, mere shoves. The difference was that for a trained person time moved more slowly. He was past the last patrolman and out when he felt a sting in the small of his back. He knew it could not be one of the officer's guns because there was not enough impact. He turned. None of them were pointing at him. Ms. Kaufperson had gone into a flailing of the arms. Yet some one apparently had gotten off a shot at him. He was glad the little boy had not been hit. Remo moved away from the office. The body had just accepted the intrusion of the object. He would be feeling the pain soon.

Walking toward the front door, his back began to feel as if someone had stuffed a hot stove coil into it. He slowed the breathing process, and with it, the circulation. This meant that by the time he reached the taxi he was really moving slowly because the slowed blood stream slowed the legs.

"I've been wounded," he said, falling into the back seat and now, by hand, closing off the circulation to the area.

"Idiot," said Chiun, slapping Remo's hand away from the wound and inserting his own. He motioned the driver to go forward quickly. While ordinarily the driver would have told anyone fleeing that he wouldn't be part of it, he had already been educated not to argue with the Master of Sinanju.

"Idiot," said Chiun. "How could you get your-

71

self wounded to me? How could you do this thing?"

"I don't know. I was making a simple move and I felt this pain in my back."

"Simple move. Pain in the back. Were you sleeping? What were you doing?"

"I told you, a simple move. It's only a tissue wound."

"Well, at least I suppose I am to be grateful for that," said Chiun, adding in Korean that it showed incredible ingratitude for Remo to risk the destruction of all that Chiun had made of him. It was a desecration of the values of Sinanju that Remo should risk his life.

"I'll remember that, Little Father," said Remo, though he was smiling.

"It is not just another white life you are risking anymore. I hoped I had trained you out of the courage silliness of the West that leads men to ignore that most useful sense of fear."

"All right, all right. Stop carping. I don't know where I got hit from."

"Ignorance is even worse than courage."

"I don't know what happened." And in Korean because the cab driver might be listening, Remo went through, in detail, everything he did in Warner Pell's office and everything everyone else did.

"And what did the child do?" asked Remo.

"The little boy? Nothing, I think," said Remo.

"When you arranged the policemen's guns, you thought of guns. So those guns did not injure you."

"Well, one must have."

"Which?"

"I don't know."

72

"Then it was none of the policemen's guns. This is so. For many is the man who watches the sword that is killed by the rock and many who watch the rock and the sword who are killed by the club. But he who uses his full senses is not killed by the thing he watches."

"I am Sinanju. I use my full sense."

"There is an organ in the body called the grinder."

"You mean the appendix."

"We call it the grinder. Once a long time ago this organ ground coarse foods. But it no longer was needed when man began to eat simple grains. And it stopped working. Now if a man were to eat a fish with all its scales, his body would be hurt by the coarseness of it because the grinder does not work, although he still has it in his body."

"What are you saying? I need your little stories now like I need an abcess."

"You always need my little stories so you will understand."

"What does my appendix have to do with this whole thing?"

"That which is clear is clear. That which is not clear is more clear."

"Of course," said Remo. "Fish scales. It's fish scales that did it. For a minute, I thought it was a bullet in my back. I hope the worm and the hook aren't still in me."

"Ridicule is merely another way of saying something is above you."

"Beyond me."

"One should not explain the mysteries of the universe to a toad."

"Croak. Try again. Perhaps if we weren't talking Korean, you might ease up on the riddles." The pain was leaving Remo's back as Chiun's hand worked gently on the nerves surrounding the hole in his flesh.

"Riddles? To an imbecile in the dark a candle is the greatest riddle of all, for where does the dark go? This has nothing to do with the candle and all to do with the imbecile." And at this Chiun was quiet.

But Remo persisted and finally Chiun asked:

"What sense that you do not need has been turned off?"

"None."

"Wrong. It is so turned off you are not aware of it."

"Sense? Sense?"

"When you looked at the guns, what sort of things did you not look at? Things that were of no danger to you, correct? And what was of no danger to you? Do you not know what was of no danger to you? Can you think of what was of no danger to you?"

Remo shrugged.

"Was the desk of no danger to you?"

"Right. The desk."

"Was the wall of no danger to you?"

"You know I watch walls. Like you, I'm aware of walls when I enter a room."

"Correct. But not a desk. Now we both know many walls are hidden traps. But not desks, so you did not watch the desk. Who were the people in the room?"

"The two patrolmen, the two detectives, Ms. Kaufperson, and the corpse. You don't mean the corpse did it?"

Chiun sighed. "We are so lucky, so infinitely lucky that you are alive. You should be dead now."

"Who? C'mon, tell me."

"I have been telling you and what I tell you most now is that your ignorance shows how dangerous these assassins are. They are not seen. You see them but you do not see them."

"Who, dammit, who?"

"The child," said Chiun. "Think of all who have died. Were there not children at the Army post, right in the house where Kaufmann died? Yes, there were. And where was that other victim killed but in a schoolyard with children? And if this is not clear enough for even your dull eyes, how were all these people killed? By bombs which a child could throw or leave. Or with bullets of a small-caliber gun. And what angles did the bullets make into the body? Under the chin and upward, the direction a child uses. A child who could conceal a small gun but not a large one, a child whom bodyguards would only attempt to shoo away, never to protect themselves from. A child who is never noticed as a person, not even by you who was injured by one."

"Wow," said Remo.

And Chiun watched the streets of Chicago go by.

"Wow," said Remo again.

"You guys talk funny," said the cab driver. "Is it Chinese?"

"No," said Chiun. "It is language."

"What language?"

"Language," said Chiun.

"Japanese?"

75

"No. Japanese is Japanese. Language is language."

The conclusion was inescapable. All white men were dense, as dense as Chinese or Africans. Or the Koreans to the south and even those in Pyong Yang in the north. Stupid. Only Sinanju was a fitting receptacle for the light of wisdom, except of course the fishermen by the docks and the woodworkers and the villagers who lived off the toil of the Masters of Sinanju.

By a process of elimination, Chiun had reduced the world to the Master of Sinanju, who was worthy, and all others, who were not.

And not even all the Masters had been perfect. There was he during the reign of the Tangs who had grown corpulent and lazy, preferring to let others do his work. And one could not always believe the tales about ancestors because sometimes uncles and aunts did not portray with the greatest accuracy the accomplishments of relatives.

Even the Master who had trained Chiun to be Master had been flawed.

The thought came sadly to Chiun that there was only one person in the world whose intelligence, wisdom, and force he could admire.

And how could that person tell his pupil, Remo, that Remo might be defenseless?

CHAPTER FIVE

The bullet itself had done only minor tissue damage. In a small motel room outside Chicago, Chiun removed it with Remo's assistance. The long fingernails probed into the back. Remo eased and contracted the muscles. His face lay on a fresh white towel and he could smell the residue of detergent. The rug had been washed with an overpowering soap. His breathing was slow and meticulous and steady, to raise his pain threshhold. In this soft semi-sleep of breathing, Remo remembered the earliest training and his first life of hamburgers and sugar cola drinks and a pistol at his side when he was a patrolman in that New Jersey city before Dr. Smith's frameup had brought him to his new life.

He remembered the cool beers and the dates and the suggestions that he marry Kathy Gilhooly, whose father was a deputy inspector and who would be a perfect match for him. And how one night in the hallway of her father's house, she reached down and aroused him by hand, and told him, "When we marry, you get the real thing. I'm saving it for you, Remo."

Save it? She could keep it forever. After he was charged with killing that pusher, Inspector Gilhooly tried to get the evidence thrown out, make some deal with the prosecutor, but Smith's organization was already at work, and Gilhooly had to back off and tell his daughter to find someone else. Remo had often wondered what had happened to her, if she had gotten that two-family house with a husband, the half-carat ring with four children, and the new color television set every five years. A bar in the basement was her big ambition, and maybe if Remo had become a chief, then a summer home in Spring Lake, New Jersey, with the politicians. The Shore.

Remo felt the bullet go. Oh, what great hand and what great eye can frame thy fearful symmetry? He had lost that life and been granted in return more than two thousand years of human genius, one with a tradition of self-power so old it undoubtedly preceded the written word.

Chiun told tales of the first master who plied his fearsome art. How the flaming circle had come down from the heavens and told the first Master of Sinanju that there were better ways to use his body and his mind. Before the written word. What great hand and what great eye can frame thy fearful symmetry? Chiun's hands massaged the wound, and Remo brought himself down farther into his mind where he could feel the blood move in every vein and artery. Yogas did this, but

78

Sinanju was older than yoga, old as the first bands that plucked the wild rice from the marshy swamp where lumbering dinosaurs plodded their last days as crawly little men prepared to take over the world. Was it that old? No, not that old. The inked printed words in all the books Remo could find told him 2,800 B.C.

Old. Old as his heart, which now rested on that single beat, his body not needing blood. Hold. In the dark white light, hold. Still. One with all being.

And beat. Once. Slowly again and up, up from the mind. Up from Kathy Gilhooly, whose white gloves covered the hands that did the job in lieu of the marriage contract and the real thing. "Remo, I promise. I can't wait for your body."

Old. Older than the waking sun. The sun source of all. Sinanju and the rug smelled again of violent soap and the towel of its detergent and he was in a motel room and Chiun clinked a small metal object into a glass ashtray. Remo looked up. It was the bullet.

"Your body did not even catch it as it should have. It tore right through tissue," said Chiun.

"I wasn't expecting it."

"That you do not need to tell me. I saw," said Chiun. The long white fingernails were clean. "I hate bullets. With guns, as we feared, every man becomes his own assassin."

"You know, Little Father, sometimes when I go deep into mind, I wonder whether we should bother with being assassins."

"That, of course, is the danger of the deep mind, but do not worry. It passes."

Remo stretched and breathed and finally drank

a glass of water. Someone was training those kids to be killers. He had thought it was Pell but now Pell was dead. There was someone. Find the someone, take apart his organization and call it a day. The big thing had been solved. The *how*. It had been kids.

Funny, none of them had talked by now. The training must have included that. Well, Remo had one lead. The boy who had taken a shot at him. The boy with Ms. Kaufperson. Funny name, Kaufperson.

"Beware," said Chiun as Remo reached the door. "Beware of children."

"Kids?"

"Have you ever fought a child?"

"Not since the fifth grade," Remo said.

"Then how can you assume you can match a child? These things should not be assumed."

"I haven't come up against anything I couldn't handle, and kids are weaker than everything I have handled. Therefore, Little Father, with great courage I go risking the playpen."

"Fool," said Chiun.

"I don't understand."

"Just do not go squandering this precious gift given you, lo, these many years. Do not assume."

"All right, Little Father. If it will make you happier, I will not assume."

There was only one Kaufperson in the Chicago directory. Remo assumed it was the person he wanted. The listing followed a multitude of Kaufmans and Kaufmanns. Two N's meant German descent and one N Jewish, usually. If that was so, were there German Kaufpersonns?

Roberta Kaufperson lived in a modern highrise

with new carpeting, fresh-painted walls, and two patrolmen guarding her apartment. He moved back behind a corner as soon as he saw the uniforms. He entered a doorway marked Exit which led to a stairwell. He climbed twelve more flights of stairs until he was on the roof, then figuring just about which area would be directly above Ms. Kaufperson's apartment, he slipped over the small metal guardrail, caught an edge with one hand, popped out free, caught a window ledge again, popped out, one catch, one pop, twelve times going down and there was the back of the brunette Afro pointed at a television set showing "Sesame Street," up and lift the window, into the apartment, catch the vocal cords in the left hand and:

"Don't be afraid, Ms. Kaufperson, I'm not going to hurt you. I'm here to help you. But you've got to tell the policemen at the door to go away. Nod if you will do this."

Terror in the gray blue eyes. But the Afro trembled in a nod. Remo released the pressure from the vocal cords. Trembling, Ms. Kaufperson stood up, a full-bodied woman with a good even walk. Remo stayed close to her as she went to the door.

She pressed a speaker button.

"Thank you for waiting," she said. "I'll be all right now."

"You made enough stink to get us here. You sure you don't want us to stay?"

"Positive."

"Okay. But would you call the captain back at the station? He's got to approve it."

"Certainly."

As if moving with computer rhythms, she

walked to the telephone, dialed the emergency number of the police department, briefly argued with someone on the other end as to whether she would dial another number for the captain, waited, told someone to remove the two patrolmen, hung up, and shouted:

"It's all right. Get out of here."

"Yes, Ma'am."

Remo heard the officers trudge away down the hall. Ms. Kaufperson removed her blouse with a wild uplift over her head. Her breasts strutted forth erect, with nipples hardened to attention.

"What's that about?" asked Remo.

"Aren't you going to rape me?"

"No."

"You didn't swing down some rope and risk your life just to say hello."

"I want information."

"Then you're not going to rape me?"

"No."

"Are you queer?"

"No," said Remo.

"Then how can you stand there?"

"I'm just standing. I don't know what you're talking about."

"You look at a half-naked woman and you're not excited?"

"I don't mean to be insulting, but there isn't a woman I'd climb down a building for."

"You *are* queer. Maybe you want a meaningful relationship. But don't think I'm going to give you a deep significant part of myself just because you climbed in a window. Sex is one thing. My soul is another."

"You can keep both," Remo said.

"I thought you were shot," Ms. Kaufperson said. "That's it, isn't it? You're wounded and too weak for sex."

"Right," said Remo. "Couldn't possibly hack it."

He saw her nipples ease out and the breasts become loose. She put her shirt back on.

"Then I don't hold it against you."

"Good," said Remo. "I want to know about that kid you came into the office with today. Who is he? What's his name? Where does he live?"

"I'm not permitted to give out that information."

"I'm going to get it," said Remo.

"I don't know where that child lives. This was his final day in school. His family moved and he was transferring. I think he went to New York."

"Terrific," Remo said.

"New York or Los Angeles," said Ms. Kaufperson. "I really don't remember."

"Great," Remo said. "Let's try this one then. The kid who was in the office when Pell got shot. Who is he?"

"I'm not permitted to give out that information, I told you."

"And I told you I'm going to get it."

"Then take it," she said and she flaunted her chest, resting her hands on her strong hips, whose outlines thrust wide through the coarse woven shirt. Remo could smell her wanting him and he pressed her to him and carried her to the blue-and-white Rya rug on the floor, where his hands busied themselves under her skirt, bringing her close to the edge but not over.

"The name of the kid," whispered Remo.

"Give it to me, you bastard, give it to me."

"Give me what I want."

"You bastard," she groaned, soft whines coming from her throat, her groin moving in want, ready for him.

"The name," said Remo.

"Alvin Dewar, nine, 54 Wilton Street, an underachiever. Give it to me, you bastard."

And with the slow meticulous grace of his body, Remo put the groaning, crying woman over the edge, *Padoom*. She dug her nails into his back and pressed him to her with her legs, pressing, praying he would again and he did again, wonderful.

"Oh, that was good. Goody, good, good," she said. "What's your name?"

"Remo."

"I love that name. What's your last name?"

"Spit."

"What a fantastic sexy name. Remo Spit."

"I've got to go. Thanks for the name."

"Wait. Do you want his file? I know everything about that Dewar kid. He's what we call a peer-alienated functioner."

"What's that?"

"A shithead who can't get along with anyone else."

"I've got to go."

"I'll go with you."

"I work alone," Remo said.

"You don't go unless I say so."

Remo smiled and gave her a kiss on the cheek.

"Bye," he said.

He felt her lock her ankles. She smiled.

"See if you can get out," she said. "I have extraordinary muscle control everywhere. Over all my body. Don't be frightened if you can't remove yourself. Some men panic and hurt themselves. Go ahead. Try."

What Ms. Kaufperson knew was a simple double pin that used her legs on the small of Remo's back to pull him into her.

"No one's ever been able to break it," said Ms. Kaufperson, a bubble gum grin spread on a whipped cream happy face.

With two light presses into her throat, Remo popped out.

"Ooooh, that was good. In many ways," said Ms. Kaufperson.

There was something strange about the apartment that Remo could not quite fathom. It was a modern design, with chrome lights butting into black-and-white leather furniture, thick rugs and paintings framed in gold wire that looked like smears surrounded by gold braid. Incense wafted from five silver goblets. The chairs looked like polished sculpture with small leather pads for those who were able to figure out they were chairs. Something was wrong about this place and Ms. Kaufperson.

"You've got to let me go with you. I can tell you all about the Dewar kid."

Remo shrugged. "C'mon. Get dressed and we'll go."

As soon as her skirt was buttoned around her waist, Sashur—as she loudly proclaimed her new name—expounded on her ability to cope with the inferior male psyche. "For thousands of years, men have used women as sexual objects. Now it's our turn. You're just a thing to me."

"What was your old name?" asked Remo.

"You mean my male-oppressed name?"

"Yeah."

"Roberta Kaufmann."

"Were you ever married to an accountant?"

"Yes. A pig. He's dead."

"How recent?"

"Couple of days ago. Probably murdered by the capitalist conspiracy of which he was such a grubby part."

"You seem to do all right."

"Only because I won't accept the slave life given me."

The building had a concierge at a little desk, who told Ms. Kaufperson that "that person is waiting outside."

"Jeezus H. Christ," said Ms. Kaufperson. "He hangs in there like a toothache."

Remo and Sashur took an elevator to the downstairs garage.

"We'll have to use my car. I wanted to cab it. No parking places in this city. But I'll drive. I hate to bring a car into a socio-economically deprived neighborhood where the oppressed lumpenproletariat will express their struggle for freedom against even such symbols as a car."

"What?" Remo asked.

"Niggers steal hubcaps."

"I thought this Dewar kid was white."

"He is. He lives in a highrise, but it's near a slum. Not like this."

"What's this place cost a month to live?" asked Remo.

"It's a ripoff. Fifteen hundred a month."

"You do that on a teacher's salary?"

"Of course not. You don't think a society as corrupt as this would allow a teacher such luxurious surroundings."

"How do you afford it?"

"I told you. I found a way."

"What way?"

"I have my own liberated way that's none of your male business."

"I think it is," Remo said. At first, she thought he was going to make love to her in the elevator but when the pain became great she knew there was something else.

"The money. Where did you get the money?" Remo asked.

"Divorce settlement. Fathead was loaded."

Remo released the grip.

"I bet you're happy now, Pig," said Sashur, rubbing her elbow. "Now you know, so flaunt it. In this oppressed society that's the only way for a woman to make money, bastard. What're you, a sadist or something?"

"A sadist likes pain," Remo said. "Therefore he is sloppy because he has no purpose in his causing of pain." And he explained to her that pain was actually the body working well and should be used as a signal device for the mind. The problem with most people was that they ignored the first gentle signals until it was too late and all they had left was strong useless pain.

"You like pain, you mother, you try this," said Sashur, and with the toe of her Gucci sandal, sent a wide screaming kick toward Remo's groin. It struck nothing, and as the elevator door opened, Remo helped her to her feet.

87

She swung at his head and missed. She kicked at his stomach and missed.

"All right, you win," she said.

In the silver Mercedes sports coupe, littered with pamphlets about the oppression of the poor, she insisted that Remo fasten his safety belt. He said he was safer floating free. She said no one was going anywhere without the safety belt fastened. Remo consented. He could still survive a crash, even with a locked safety belt.

Snap went the belt. *Swish* went Sashur's right hand down on Remo's strapped midsection. *Owwww* went Sashur's mouth when she met a knuckle coming up.

"Animal," she said and gunned the Mercedes up the ramp to the fading sunlight of a Chicago evening, the evening spread in rich red colors, largely the reflection from tiny pollution particles in the air.

At a red traffic light, she moaned.

"Lights bother you?" Remo asked.

"No. He's going to get us now."

Behind him, Remo saw a balding man in a gray suit dash from Sashur's building like he was going over hot coal barefoot. He skittered around an oncoming taxi whose tires squealed, burning asphalt and rubber in an effort not to put him away, midsection.

"It's nothing, George," yelled Sashur as the man's reddened twisted face intruded itself into the driver's window. "It's strictly a platonic relationship. You're so damned jealous it's sickening, George. George, meet Remo. Remo, meet George, who thinks I sleep with every man I meet."

"You can't do this to me," said George.

"You're incredible. The male psyche is not to be believed."

"Why did you try to avoid me?"

"Why? Why? Because of just this kind of scene. Just think of this kind of suspicious jealous scene."

"I'm sorry."

"You're always sorry, and you do it just the same."

"You know how difficult Justice is sometimes."

"Go away," Sashur said. Bang. George's head knocked against the oncoming window. Sashur gunned the Mercedes through the red light.

"Creep. He drives me up a wall. The male mind is so suspicious."

Remo flicked her right hand off his thigh.

"I wasn't going to hit."

"I know that," Remo said. "What'd he mean about justice being difficult?"

"Who knows? Who cares?"

In a plush white twenty-two-story building, set like white marble in a field of ghetto mud, the doorman halted Ms. Kaufperson and Remo. They had to be announced.

"Alvin is not here," came the fuzzy voice through the little speaker.

"Tell her it's all right. Ms. Kaufperson is here," she said to the doorman.

"It's a Miss Kaufperson," the doorman said.

"Wait a minute, doorperson," said Sashur. "It's not Miss Kaufperson, it's Miz Kaufperson."

"It's Mizzzz Kaufperson," the doorman said.

"Alvin still isn't home," came the voice.

89

"Tell her we want to speak to her anyway," said Remo.

"Well, all right. If you want to," came the voice over the speaker. "Alvin isn't in trouble again, is he?"

"No, no," said Sashur Kaufperson. "It's all right."

In the elevator Remo asked her why she hadn't just changed her name to Smith or Jones.

"I wanted to liberate the *Kauf* from the *Mann*. Give a new perspective to the horizons in which women may see themselves."

No, Remo didn't want to do it in the elevator, even though they had all of twenty floors to go and had wasted two of them already.

"That's the penthouse," said Remo. "What's a public school kid doing living in a penthouse? With all that money, you'd think his folks would send him to a private school."

"Some parents will spend money on all sorts of material things. But never on the important things."

At the penthouse, Alvin Dewar greeted them himself with a lovely material thing. He held a silver-plated .25 caliber Beretta, and it was pointed up at Remo's throat.

Remo felt Ms. Kaufperson pressing to leave, pushing behind him, pushing him out into the barrel of the gun. She had insisted that the old formality of the woman leaving the elevator first be abandoned as the patronizing vestige of sexism it was. So Remo was in the elevator door, facing this peer-alienated functioner with a pistol.

And it should have been no trouble at all, except Remo could not strike, could not injure the boy. His muscles would not move on this four-foot-seven-inch ninety-pound alienated functioner.

The kid was going to kill him.

CHAPTER SIX

Remo saw the little pink index finger tighten on the trigger, and while his own body could not advance on an attack, it could move away. Remo's left hand snaked behind him to Sashur Kaufperson's waist, and using the weight of her body and his, he split them both so, like two pendulums colliding, they each bounced to opposite sides of the elevator and the .25 caliber slug plinked into the new polished wood of the wall. It dug a neat dark hole. So did the next. And three others. The elevator door closed. The last shot hit the outside with the sound of a dish breaking on one sharp rock.

Remo was up and helping Sashur to her feet.

"He has hostile tendencies," she said. "I guess he has difficulties relating to extracurricular visits."

"He's a killer," said Remo, pressing the "open"

button. He was shaken. His body had never failed to respond before, but unless the gun had a seventh bullet, he was in no danger. The door opened. Another little dark hole appeared in the polished wood of the elevator wall. Seven bullets.

"Fucking kid is a killer," said Ms. Kaufperson, noticing a hole through her Gucci blouse.

Alvin was fast in his sneakers. He threw the gun wildly away as he turned a corner. Remo was around the corner with him in a loping shuffle. Alvin tried to run behind a man built like a wide landslide, a mountain of a landslide. His forearms were almost as big as Remo's neck.

"Hey, you, leave my kid alone."

His massive weight balanced evenly on size fourteen shoes. He stuck out an arm confidently as if it were a wall against this thin fellow following his son. His eyes teared just slightly as his rib cage collapsed into his lower intestines. His sphincters released his digested breakfast into his pants. He decided standing was too much for what was left of his body so he collapsed to the light maroon carpeting of the hallway.

Remo was into the apartment proper after Alvin. A bleached blonde, with hair in silver curlers, tried to shut the door. The door bounced back into her face.

Alvin made it to the bathroom, locking it behind him. He saw the lock pop out in a halo of splinters onto the white tile floor.

"Hello, Alvin," said Remo, cornering him in the bathtub. He wanted, at least, just to slap the kid but the hand that could become a shatterer of molecule chains could not move. So Remo looked menacing. In all his training, he had never learned to look fearsome. Everything was aimed at appearing harmless, even through the hit. He even stood with great quiet. His body was quiet. He menaced with his voice. It worked, and the shattered lock on the floor didn't hurt any either.

"You're in trouble."

"Dad!" yelled Alvin.

"He's not going to help."

"Mom," yelled Alvin.

"She's not going to help."

"Ms. Kaufperson."

"Coming, Alvin. Don't be afraid," yelled Sashur.

"Be afraid," said Remo.

"You can't hurt me," said Alvin.

"What makes you think so?"

"There are laws," said Alvin.

"Alvin, you have two seconds to tell me who gave you the order to hit Pell. Or your head goes like this." Remo put his hand on a round polished edge of an aquamarine sink and squeezed off a piece like a chunk of bread.

"There, Alvin, imagine it's your head," said Remo, bluffing.

"Ms. Kaufperson," cried Alvin, terror widening his eyes as Sashur came into the bathroom.

"Ms. Kaufperson isn't going to help you," said Remo.

"Alvin, you're in big legal trouble," said Ms. Kaufperson.

"Let me handle this," said Remo.

"No comment," said Alvin.

"I'm going to bring him to the police station," said Ms. Kaufperson.

"Who gave you the gun, Alvin?"

"We ought to let the police do this, Remo. So they'll have a case."

Ms. Kaufperson took Alvin firmly by the wrist, reaching in past Remo, who blocked the doorway. She yanked Alvin with her. Remo followed them out of the apartment and out of the building, and when he saw her enter the police station, with the surly tyke, he let them go. Fine. She would tell the police to check him out in the killing of Warner Pell, the youngster would put the police onto who had trained him and paid him so well, the cops would round up the other kids—there had to be others with simultaneous killings—and with the new killers gone, Smitty's program of protected witnesses would pick up again.

The air tasted of the soot and filth of millions of people living close, burning things to heat themselves, discarding garbage, and rushing. You could feel people rush. And Remo didn't care whether the Constitution worked or Smith's operation worked or about anything to do with why he had accepted that offer to join so many years before. Then why was he doing it? Why did he continue?

On this hot night, the buildings seemed to sweat black faces from open windows. A white man walking through this neighborhood alone attracted chuckles. A few glistening fat women called out that whitey ought to start running and that if he didn't run now he would be running mighty soon, heh, heh.

Why did he continue: Why? And the only answer was as true as it was confusing. He did it because it was what he did.

Government came and went, civilizations rose

and then left their buried droppings for later civilizations to try to figure out, but Sinanju, this better use of the human mind and body, continued. That was eternal because it was rooted in the best of what man could be. New governments only promised the best, like some hope that always ended with a new dictator replacing the one before him. What Smith was fighting was not chaos or disorder or elements that prevented good, honest government. He was fighting human nature. And Remo, serving him, was using that same human nature to the fullest. Was he becoming too much like Chiun? Would he end up thinking of himself as the world's only human being, with a bunch of lessers running around polluting the landscape?

"Good evening, honkey," said a thin black face atop a muscular body. Several people lounging on stoops chuckled.

"Speedy's got the honkey," laughed a woman. "Come see Speedy. He gone do the job on the honkey. Run, honkey. Honkey ain't runnin'."

Perhaps Chiun was right. Yet sometimes Remo felt that Chiun's personality ran alongside the wisdom of Sinanju. Chiun was Chiun and Sinanju was Sinanju, and while Sinanju was most of him, it was not all of him. Chiun might have been a *kvetch* in any age.

"You run?" said the thin black face.

And yet who was Remo? How much of him was Sinanju?

"You need a stickin', honkey."

A small glistening knife caught the glint of an overhead street light. It was coming toward Remo. He took the hand on the knife and put it into the right eye of the thin black face. And left it there, neat, in the brain.

Was Remo running alongside Sinanju also? Was he a visitor in his own body?

A lumbering hulk, with a large two-by-four swinging around him like a baseball bat looking to connect with Remo's head, plodded into Remo's path. Now here was a perfect example. Remo saw the man slower than he was actually moving. He saw the two-by-four moving so slowly he could have carved his initials on it.

Sinanju controlled his eyesight. He didn't. He breathed this way, he saw that way, he heard this way. Who was he anymore?

Remo split the big board precisely and let the mocha-colored man go *whoomphing* into a stoop.

He couldn't even slap a kid who was going to kill him. Now if it were up to him, he would have slapped. And he wanted to. But his body wouldn't do it. Sinanju wouldn't let his body.

A pistol cocked across the street. Now here was another good case. He heard this small sound clearly. It was distinguished from the car engines and the shouts and the footsteps and the windows opening down the block. It was clear and his mind picked it up, separated it, and labeled it "menace" without his even trying. Even without his consent.

The sound came from behind a stoop fifteen yards up to the right. Two bodies, heavy, probably male, came puffing up behind him. Remo lowered slightly, moving back and taking his two arms as scythes upended two men in blue jean jackets with the words "Spade Stones" sewn across the shoulders.

97

"He bruised a Stone," yelled someone.

The pistol, like a silver jewel in a fat black hand, appeared from behind the stoop. Remo pushed it backward into a mouth that finally opened to the pressure on it.

And another good case. This man couldn't control the reflex action of his trigger finger. It closed. The bullet came out his right ear with waxy sediment, tiny hairs and a spray of brain. Now this man's reflexes were reflexes. Remo's were a tradition. He didn't even have control of his reflexes. They were Sinanju.

It was a question of soul. His body and his mind belonged to Sinanju. His soul belonged to him, and just as Chiun would have been a carper in any age, Remo would be a questioner, and the question would always be: Why am I doing this? And the answer would always be: Because this is what I do.

In terror, a Spade Stone trying to flee Remo got himself trapped between Remo and a corner of the stoop.

"Leave me alone," said Remo. "I've got problems to work out."

The man was agreeable. He fell over himself agreeing. He made a whoooping dash across the sidewalk, over a fire hydrant, and skittered around a white Eldorado pimpmobile, where he hid.

It occurred to Remo on his thoughtful walk down the block that if people could just express themselves, this whole racial problem in America could be solved. All he had said was he had problems and would the man leave him alone. And the man had. One human being responding to another. It was good to get mutual concern back in America.

When he reached the motel, Chiun's daytime TV soaps were ending, and Remo waited quietly as Warner Hemper explained to Dr. Theresa Lawson Cook, for the sixth time in the day's episode, that an ecological abortion could not save Mrs. Cortina Woolets in her religious revival backed by the Mafia, even though the father of the unborn child was a Vietnamese refugee.

"Trash," said Chiun, when the commercial ended.

"Trash," he said again and set the taping machine atop the television to begin its recording of the other two network channels the next day.

"Then why don't you stop watching them?" Remo asked.

Chiun looked loftily at Remo.

"How dare you begrudge an old and gentle creature his brief moments of joy? You are troubled."

"Yeah. I've been thinking. Something strange happened today."

"With a child," said Chiun.

"You know," Remo said.

"I knew."

"Why did it happen like that? I was powerless, and this kid was going to kill me."

"Not powerless," said Chiun. "Are you not alive?"

"Well, I am alive, yes."

"That is the most necessary power. The ability to bring harm to others is secondary."

"What if I had been in a position where my

only out was hitting the kid was who holding the gun on me?"

Chiun nodded and thought a moment. His longer fingernails slid together like the joining of delicately polished curved ivory needles.

"But that did not happen, did it?"

"No, it didn't," said Remo. He looked at a watch on the wall. It was a minute and a half late. In seventeen minutes, the line to Smith would be open.

"There are many explanations for what happened to you, all of them true," said Chiun. "As you know, Sinanju is a poor village."

"I know, I know, I know, I know. You had to rent out your services to the emperors of the world so the children of Sinanju wouldn't starve. I know."

"And the babies during time of famine had to be put into the cold waters of the bay. Therefore any failure of a mission is really killing the children we serve. This has been so, lo, these many years, lo, these many generations, lo, even unto centuries."

"I know, I know, I know."

"He who thinks he knows before he hears does not know."

"I know," said Remo.

"Listen."

"I'm listening."

"You are not."

"All right. I'm listening."

"Now you are," Chiun said. "Children are promises of greatness, in all manners possible. They have all been made holy in your eyes, not just the babes of Sinanju but all children."

"So?" said Remo. He tried to slump into a chair but it came out as a delicate, precise placement of his body with the chair.

"So you cannot kill hope. And this is a good thing. What has been given us is a power that we achieve by giving ourselves."

"That's right. And I don't exist anymore. That framed killing has finally worked. Patrolman Remo Williams is dead. I don't know who I am now."

"You are a better you. Why, sometimes," Chiun said solemnly, "you remind me of myself. But do not think this is all the time. You had much to overcome."

"I liked what it was I overcame."

"You liked living with your mind and body asleep?"

"Sometimes, all I want to do is go into a bar and get a hamburger, yes, meat, and a beer, and get fat and maybe marry Kathy Gilhooly."

"What is a Kooly Gilloolly?"

"Kathy Gilhooly. A girl I once knew in Newark."

"How long ago?"

"Ten years at least. No. Twelve. Twelve years, I think."

"She is dead twice. Do not think you can ever find her. Every five years, a white person changes. If you see her, you will kill her in your eyes, that last remembrance of what you once loved. Wrinkles and fat will bury it, tiredness in the eyes will smother it, and in her place will be a woman. The girl dies when the woman emerges."

It was still six minutes until the call to Smith

and Remo got up without answering and walked toward the kitchen.

"What rudeness is this that you inflict silence between us?" said Chiun.

"I'm sorry, I . . ."

But Chiun now turned in silence and went triumphantly into the kitchen. If someone was to not speak to the other, it would be the Master of Sinanju not speaking to his pupil, not the reverse. Besides, Remo would soon resolve his problems. In his new life, Remo was really only at puberty. A difficult time for anyone.

"Arrogant," said the pupil in American.

Chiun chose not to be offended, since the silence was his and he was not about to give it up for a minor rebuke.

At the precisely proper time, Smitty picked up the telephone and Remo told him everything was being resolved legally. There was this group that was using kids to kill which explained why no one had seen the killers. Grownups ignored children, especially at a murder scene.

"I know all about it," Smith said. "I think you've got everything solved but the problem."

"The Chicago police have a kid. He's one of them. He'll spill his little head open and the whole system will go down constitutionally. You ought to like that."

"Except for one thing, Remo."

"What's that?"

"I've already heard from Chicago. Little Alvin Dewar admits that he shot Warner Pell. He said Pell was sexually assaulting him and he grabbed the gun from Pell's desk to defend himself."

"He's lying. Get the cops to beat it out of him."

"Good thought, except our little Alvin Dewar has a bank account of $50,000 waiting for him. You know what the law is. He'll be out in no more than twenty-four months. He'll be a rich kid on his way to becoming a rich man."

"That's not my problem. Change the legal system," Remo said.

"And another thing," Smith said. "We still don't know how they get the locations of the hidden witnesses for their hits. There's still a leak someplace in the government. And another thing. Why did you go after Pell when I told you to wait?"

"I wanted to wrap this up," said Remo.

"Yes," said Smith drily. "And now Pell, our only real lead, is dead."

"Maybe what Alvin said is true. Maybe Pell was trying to mash him. Sure, that's probably what happened. Pell was the boss and now he's dead. And as long as we're complaining, how was it that the Chicago cops recognized me today and tried to arrest me?"

"Were you hurt?" asked Smith.

"No. Just a bullet in the back," said Remo with a grim satisfaction. "How about how that happened?"

"I'm afraid the Justice Department put out a wire on you and Chiun regarding forged credentials. It happened before I could stop it."

"Yeah," said Remo. "See. Nobody's perfect."

"No, you're not," said Smith calmly. "At any rate, I hope you don't have any more such trouble. But the problem still remains. We don't know—and I mean *know*, not guess—who's been behind the kids, and we don't know who the leak is in the government, and we don't know anything about the organization of the kids, and until you put that all together, this job is still going on. Goodbye."

The phone went dead and Remo hurriedly dialed to tell Smith he couldn't do the job; he couldn't go up against kids. But all he got was a busy signal.

"Little Father," he said to Chiun. "I need your help."

There was silence from the kitchen.

"I'm sorry. All right? Are you happy? I've got to find an answer to this kid thing. Help me, please."

Chiun returned to the living room of the motel suite. He nodded softly.

"What did you mean by arrogant?" he said.

CHAPTER SEVEN

Major General William Tassidy Haupt was on the move. His forces were rolling and he knew one word: "Attack."

"We'll hit those fuckers with everything we've got. They'll think they've run into a battery of Horlands."

"Howitzers," said a young lieutenant, just out of the Point, who had actually fired one during training—a fact that prompted Haupt's chief of staff to ask if they sounded as loud as they looked in the movies.

"Louder," said the lieutenant.

"Will you two shut up? This is a strategy session," said General Haupt. "What are you talking about?"

"Nothing, sir. The audio effect of a Howitzer."

"This is a strategy meeting of an American Army command, Lieutenant, I do not wish to hear one word out of you about Horlands, tanks, pistols, grenades, rockets and all the folderol they like to talk about at the Point. Here we separate the men from the boys. You want to play games, you go to some combat outfit and stay a second lieutenant all your life. You want to dig in and be real Army, you guts it up with everyone else and prepare for the press conference."

"Press conference," gasped the chief of staff.

"No choice," said General Haupt coldly. "Our backs are to the wall. We win or die. Options limited. Therefore, at eighteen hundred hours I have summoned the three networks, Associated Press, and United Press International to be here."

Men checked their watches. Haupt's chief of staff exhaled a large gust of air. "The balloon is up," he whispered to the lieutenant.

"The problem is this," Haupt said, going to a large chart at the back of the briefing room. "One: A Martin Kaufmann has been killed while on our post. Two: While his safety was the responsibility of Fort Dix personnel, and so publicly acknowledged, I have received a call indicating some effort will be made to hold us responsible. Three: The caller had access to personal information about my life, leading me to believe it is either the Justice Department or the Central Intelligence Agency. I recommend at the press conference we announce that it is a major government agency and allow the press to assume it is the CIA."

"What if the CIA fights back?" asked the chief of staff.

"In its present position, I do not believe it is capable of launching a major attack. The hidden armor, Colonel, is that the CIA will not really be in a position to do anything except deny the charge which we are not making in the first place. We're just saying 'major government agency.' By this action I hope to convince the caller that he can't push us wherever he likes."

"And where is that, sir?" asked the lieutenant.

"Into some kind of detective work. Our caller seems to believe that we could solve the question of Kaufmann's death if we tried. However, I need not tell you what that might lead to. Once we allow ourselves to be saddled with that responsibility, and then fail in it, we are finished. We have another hidden weapon. That major agency has two men it wishes to protect, an Oriental and a caucasian who were here with Kaufmann."

"And the weapon, sir?"

"Those two persons. It is obvious they are undercover of some sort. Well, we are going to attack. I have had the post art department do these sketches of the two and I'm going to put the pictures on national television and let their agency —which will remain nameless since I don't know for sure who it is—run for cover. Run for cover, gentlemen."

He held up the two sketches.

"That doesn't look much like the two men," his chief of staff said. "I saw them while they were here."

"It doesn't matter," said Haupt. "We don't want anything to happen to those men necessarily; we just want their agency off our backs. And this will get them off. We're going to turn this thing around as quickly as a Howitzer charging

107

across an open field. Did I get the name right, lieutenant?"

"Yessir, general, yessir," said the lieutenant.

"Good. Just wanted to show you that an Army career does not limit a man to one narrow line of work," said Major General William Tassidy Haupt with a chuckle.

CHAPTER EIGHT

The Chicago Juvenile Correctional Center.

The sign was a small brass plate next to the front door of the old four-story brick building in a dismally dark section of the city, as if that narrowed it down any.

"What is it, this correctional center?" Chiun asked.

"A reform school," said Remo. He was looking at the walls of the building. The drainpipe would be all right.

"Ah, very good," said Chiun. "He tells me a reform school. As if I am supposed to know what a reform school is."

"A reform school is where they send bad kids to make them worse." If the drainpipe wasn't strong enough, there was a setback section of wall between two columns of windows, a depression running from the base of the building to the roof.

109

A man could walk up the wall there, bracing his hands against the two jut-outs of wall on either side.

"There are no bad children," said Chiun.

"Thank you, Father Flanagan. Sweet little Alvin wasn't firing that gun at you."

"That is of no moment to this discussion," Chiun said. "There are no bad children."

"Just bad parents?" The set-in wall between the windows was probably the best bet. Alvin was on the fourth floor of the building.

"Not even that," said Chiun.

Remo turned to Chiun. "All right, then, since you seem determined to tell me anyway. There aren't bad kids and there aren't bad parents. What are there then? That little punker was shooting at me."

Chiun raised a finger. "There are bad societies. This one. Children reflect what they learn, what they see, what they are. This is a bad society."

"And Korea's a good one, I suppose."

"How quickly you learn when you wish to," said Chiun. "Yes, Korea is a good one. The ancient land of the pharaohs, that was another. They knew how to treat children and surround them with beauty."

"Egypt kept slaves, for crying out loud. They were always at war."

"Yes. See. A child will remember a good example. A bad example will make a bad child." Chiun folded his arms, as if resting his case on a monumental base of logic.

Remo shook his head. So much for Chiun as Dr. Spock. "The drainpipe or the wall?" he asked.

"That is what I mean by bad example," Chiun

110

said. "Look for hard where there is easy. It is the nature of your kind."

Chiun walked away and Remo mumbled, "Carp, carp, carp," before following the old man across the street, glistening from the late night Chicago rain. How unlike New York, Remo thought—New York, where the streets never glistened in the rain because the clumps of garbage in the streets broke up the reflections from the street lights.

"This is a nice city," said Chiun, walking up the steps of the old building.

"I read all about it. It's run by a tyrant."

"I knew there was something about it I liked," Chiun said. "The tyrants were very good to work for. Greece never amounted to anything when it fell into democracy."

The uniformed guard at the desk inside the front door listened politely when Chiun said that he wanted to see . . . "What is his name, Remo?"

"Alvin Dewar."

"Alvin Dewar," Chiun said to the guard. "He is a very close relative of mine."

Chiun turned and winked at Remo broadly.

"That's strange," said the guard. "He's white, and you're Oriental."

"I know. Everyone is not lucky."

"He's a relative by marriage," Remo explained.

"That is right. Alvin is married to my daughter. He is my nephew."

"Son-in-law," Remo corrected, with an uncomfortable smile.

"He's just a kid. He can't be married to anybody," said the guard.

"Why are you being difficult?" Chiun asked. "I

come here to see my close relative ... what is his name again, Remo?"

"Alvin."

"I come here to see my very close relative, Alvin, the husband of my daughter, and you give me difficulty."

"Yeah? Well, let me tell you something. You'd be amazed at the perverts we get hanging around here, because of these little kids. Now I think you better get out of here before I call the cops. You want to see Alvin, you come tomorrow."

"Remo. Reason with him."

When the guard was asleep, Remo took his keys and Chiun led the way to the elevator.

"Perhaps it is your haircut," Chiun said.

"Perhaps what is my haircut?"

"The reason that person thought you might be a pervert. Perhaps you should see about getting a haircut."

The elevator opened onto a long corridor at the end of which sat another uniformed guard.

"Now let me handle this," Chiun said.

"Fine," said Remo. "But clean up your own bodies."

"There will be no bodies. I will trick him."

Chiun walked gently up to the desk, with Remo behind him. In back of the desk, the guard rolled away slightly in his swivel chair to free his gun hand. He was reading a copy of *Amazing Detective* stories.

"Hi, fella," said Chiun with a smile. "I gave up my Monday night football to come here to visit with my close relative, Alvin something."

"This is Wednesday," said the guard. "Who let you up here?"

112

"The kindly gentleman downstairs," Chiun said.

"Rocco? Rocco let you up here?"

"He did not tell me his name. Did he tell you his name, Remo?"

"No. But he looked like Rocco."

"Where's your pass?" said the guard.

"Remo, give him our pass."

"Yeah. Right. The pass."

When the second guard had joined Rocco in repose, Remo asked Chiun if he had any other clever schemes in mind.

"No. Everything seems to have gone along nicely. As I told you, there is no need to difficultize problems."

"There's no such word as 'difficultize.' "

"There should be."

On the wall next to the sleeping guard were long rows of shelves with papers, forms, office supplies, towels, sheets, pillowcases, and light blue uniforms. Remo took two of the sheets.

Alvin Dewar had had no trouble falling asleep. He slept the blissful sleep of a guiltless child, flat on his back, arms up over his head, sipping air through his slightly opened mouth.

"Alvinnnn. Oooooooh."

Alvin sat up on the hard-mattressed cot in the large single cell at the far end of the building, and looked toward the bars of his cell.

There were two figures there, two white swirls standing outside the bars, barely visible in the dim light from the end of the corridor.

"Alvinnnnn. Oooooohhhhh," came the call again.

Alvin rubbed the sleepers from the corners of

113

his eyes and looked again at the bars. The two figures were still there, stark white on the side near the light, black on the shadowed side away from the light.

"Who are you?" asked Alvin uncertainly.

"We are the ghosts of the men you have killed."

"How come two ghosts when I only killed one guy?" asked Alvin.

"Errrr, the spirit is divided into two parts. We are both parts."

"That's crazy," said Alvin. "Look. You want to talk to me, see my lawyer. I've got to get some sleep. There's a shrink coming tomorrow to look me over, and I want to be at the top of my form."

"We are here to give you a chance to repent of your sins."

"Hey, buddy," said Alvin. "Why don't you take your sheet and go back to the laundry? Leave me alone or I'll call a guard. I'm tired." Alvin Dewar lay back down and rolled onto his right side so he was facing the wall. He had been warned. The cops might resort to anything to get him to talk.

"Last chance, Alvin," came the voice.

"Piss off, will you?"

Alvin shook his head in disgust. Now the two dopes outside the cell were arguing.

"No such thing as a bad kid, huh?"

"He is not bad. Merely misguided." That was a funny voice, a sing-song like the Kung-fu show he used to like to watch.

Then there was a sound that Alvin didn't like, the sound of a train shrieking to a stop, metal intimidating metal. Alvin spun on his cot. His eyes were now more accustomed to the semi-dark.

There was a hole in the cell door, where one bar had been ripped loose. He saw the smaller cop in the sheet put his hands on another bar. There was that terrible metal sound again, and then the bar snapped. The little cop dropped it on the floor. The bigger cop in the sheet grabbed the cross piece that connected the upper and lower sections of bars and gave it a twist and bent it away from the door, as if it were a paper-covered wire tie for a Hefty trash bag.

Alvin Dewar suddenly came to the decision that these two were not cops. They entered his cell. Alvin sat up and pressed back toward the junction of the two walls, his back against the cold cinder block.

"You two leave me alone," he said. "I'll yell."

"Repent. Repent."

"Go away. Go away."

"Does he sound repentant to you?" the big one asked the small one.

"I am sorry to say that he does not."

"Now what are we going to do?"

"What we should have done in the first place. What everyone should have done in the first place."

And then the smaller figure in the sheet was through the ripped bars and swirling across the floor toward Alvin who pressed back harder against the wall. Rough lumps from the cinder block pressed through his thin night shirt into his back. He ignored the hurt. His mouth tasted dry. He would have liked a cigarette.

He cringed in the corner as the small figure loomed over him. Then, as if Alvin had no more weight than a feather pillow, the figure lifted him

115

and Alvin found himself lying across the sheet-clad bony knees of the apparition and being spanked.

Spanked hard.

It hurt.

"Stop. That hurts."

"It is meant to hurt, you rude and thoughtless calf," came the voice, but the sing-song no longer sang. It was a high-pitched screech.

The bigger one stood in front of Alvin as the spanking went on.

"Who told you to put the hit on Warner Pell?"

"I'm not supposed to talk," cried Alvin.

"No?" said the figure holding him. "See how you like this, calf." The spanking increased, faster and harder, like nothing Alvin had ever experienced before. If anyone had warned him there would be nights like this, he would never had gotten into the business.

"Stop it. I'll talk."

The spanking continued.

"Talk is not enough," the smaller one said. "You will go to church?"

"Yes, yes. Every Sunday. I promise."

"You will work hard in school?"

"I will. I will. I really think I like school. Stop."

"You will honor your family? Your government? Your chosen leaders?"

"Honest I will. I'm going to run for class secretary."

"Good. If you need help in convincing voters, you have only to call on me." The spanking stopped.

The bigger one said to the smaller one: "You finished?"

116

"I am done," said the smaller man, who still held Alvin across his knees.

"All right. Who told you to put the hit on Warner Pell?"

"Ms. Kaufperson. She told me to. And she made me do it. I wouldna done it any other how."

"All right," said the big one. "Alvin, if you're screwing us around, we'll be back for you. You understand that, don't you?"

"Yes, sir. I understand it. Yes, sir. Both of you, sirs. I understand. I surely do."

"Good."

Then Alvin felt himself lifted and put back on his cot and he felt a light pressure behind his ear and fell instantly asleep. In the morning, when he looked at the bars of the cell and saw them intact, he would feel that he had had a very unusual bad dream. Until he looked at the bars closely and saw rough edges on some of them where they had been ripped loose and later rejoined.

And it would ruin Alvin's taste for Maypo.

On the street outside the correctional institute, Remo walked thoughtfully along beside Chiun, kicking a can.

"One thing I don't understand, Little Father."

"One thing? If you had asked me to guess, I would have said everything. What is it, this most unusual one thing?"

"Today, I couldn't attack that kid when he was shooting at me. I couldn't lift a hand. You told me that was normal, some rigamarole about showing children only love."

"Yes? So?"

"So tonight you smacked Alvin around in that

117

cell pretty good. How come you can do it and I can't?"

"You truly wonder why there are things the Master can do and you cannot? Oh, how vainglorious are your pretensions."

"No lectures, Chiun. Why?"

"To strike a child, one must be sure that one is an adult."

"You mean I'm a child? Me? At my age?"

"In the ways of Sinanju, you are yet young."

"A child?" said Remo. "Me? Is that what you mean?"

"I mean what I mean. I do not continue explanations interminably. If I told you more, I would be carping. And I do not carp."

CHAPTER NINE

From the hallway came the sound of someone whistling. The whistler's lack of talent and the Doppler effect made the melody unrecognizable.

The whistling stopped moving. It was outside their door, and it was possible to pick out a tuneless rendition of "I Am Woman."

The key clicked in the lock, the door opened and Sashur Kaufperson entered her apartment.

Her whistling stopped somewhere in the vicinity of lifting her weary hands up to the sky, when she saw Remo and Chiun standing in the center of her living room.

She paused, then held the door open wide behind her.

"You. What do you want?"

"Talky talk," said Remo. "Close the door."

She looked at him and Remo nodded and she closed the door.

"We can start," said Remo, "with Alvin Dewar. Why did you tell him to kill Warner Pell?"

"Who told you that?"

"Alvin Dewar. Now I answered your question. You answer mine. Why did you tell the kid to kill Pell?"

Sashur glanced at her watch before walking into the living room where she sank into a chrome and velvet sofa.

"I guess I'd better tell you."

"I would recommend that," Remo said. Chiun paid no attention to the conversation. He busily scanned the walls, packed frame to frame with paintings which he thought a waste of both canvas and pigment. On the far wall, he saw a set of gold coins in a frame and walked across the room to examine them.

"I don't know," Sashur said. "Pell was in some kind of trouble. He had been doing some things with the kids. The children were becoming, well, antisocial."

"Get on with it," said Remo.

"Well, I reported Pell to the school system administration and he threatened me and ..."

"Hold it," said Remo. "That dog won't hunt. I know you and Pell were in this killer-kid operation. I know there was a lot of money involved. So don't give me any school-system crap. Start telling the truth."

"All right," Sashur said with a sigh. "I was in love with Pell. That's why I split from my husband. He tricked me into working with the kids for him. Then when my husband was killed, I met Pell and he said there was trouble, but that he had no worries. Then he said he was going to hand me up as my husband's killer. Who else had a better motive? I was still in the twerp's will. I'd wind up frying."

"That's absurd," Remo said.

"Not if you know your husband and you know all those mob people he was working for back in Detroit. I panicked, and I told Alvin to shoot Pell."

"Who was the boss of the operation?" Remo asked.

"Pell, of course."

"How was he getting the locations of the victims?"

Sashur shrugged. "I don't know. He handled all that. He just gave me the names to pass onto the kids . . . Look," she said suddenly. "It's over now. Pell is dead. Maybe I did wrong, but I did some right too, in finishing him off. Now can't you just let me be? You won't gain anything by turning me in."

Remo shook his head and noticed Sashur look at her watch, which she wore on her left wrist in a heavy leather band that would have been at home on a longshoreman.

"But you won't gain anything by putting me away," said Sashur. "I'll give you anything. Anything I have."

Chiun turned from the wall and smiled at Remo.

"How like the Western mind to think that all things and all people are for sale," he said.

"My paintings," Sashur said. She looked toward Chiun. "My collection of gold coins."

Remo shook his head.

"Just a minute, my son," said Chiun. "Some

things certainly deserve consideration. The gold coins are a pleasant offering to our house."

"No," said Remo to Chiun. "We're not dealing."

"These are good coins," said Chiun. "Of course they are behind glass and I cannot examine them closely but they are worth much if they are authentic."

"No deals."

"But surely nothing is served by turning in this gracious young lady. Is that helping the Constitution to survive?"

Sashur looked at her watch again.

"I've got to talk to Smitty," said Remo. "From you," he told Sashur, "I want a list of the names of all Pell's kids."

"I'll get it, I'll get it." Sashur stood up. "It's in the bedroom."

"Just a minute," Remo said. He walked to the door of the bedroom and looked in. The only doors belonged to closets. The only windows opened up onto thirteen stories of empty space.

"Okay, get it for me."

He left her in the bedroom and went back to the living room, where Chiun was fingering the frame of the coin collection.

"I believe there is real gold leaf used on this frame," Chiun said.

"Now listen, Chiun. We can't go around letting everybody go who offers a bribe to Sinanju."

Chiun recoiled from the frame as if it were electrically charged. "A bribe? Is that what you call an offering? A bribe?" He clapped his hand to his forehead. "My own son. Adopted, of course. A bribe."

"A bribe," said Remo. "Now no more of it.

122

We're going to get the list and then talk to Smitty before we decide what to do. He might want to handle this himself." He looked toward the bedroom. "She's taking long enough to get a list."

He approached the door just as Sashur emerged. "Here it is." She handed Remo a piece of paper with a dozen names on it. As she handed over the paper, she glanced again at her gold watch.

"These are all of them?" Remo asked.

"All I know about."

"How did they get moved around the country? Your husband was hit in North Carolina."

"Warner Pell called them class trips. Special rewards for outstanding students. He took the kids out of town himself."

"They must have been gone for days at a time. Didn't their parents ever complain?"

"Complain? Why should they complain? First of all, they are not the best of people. Second, they knew what their kids were doing, and they were getting well paid for it."

"How much?"

"Warner never told me."

"Make a guess," Remo said.

"I think the kids were getting fifty thousand dollars for each job."

"The Mafia only pays five," Remo said.

"Yeah, but Warner worked for the school system. He thought big."

"Hear that, Little Father. Fifty thousand dollars for a kid. And think of the work we do."

Chium refused to turn away from the coin collection. "Money is paper," he said. "It is not value, just a promise of value. Gold is real."

"Don't mind him," Remo told Sashur. "He's pouting."

"Are you going to turn me in?"

"Not just yet," Remo said. "Come here, I want to show you something."

He walked toward the bedroom. As Sashur followed, she said with a smile, "I'd like to show you something too."

But before she could show Remo her something, he showed her his something, which was the inside of a closet which he locked with the key.

"Why are you doing this?" she yelled through the wood-painted steel door.

"I just want you to stay put while I check this all out."

"You're a prick," she said.

"The worst," Remo agreed.

"A no-good, rotten, reneging bastard prick."

"I'd recognize myself anywhere." Remo jammed the lock of the closet door for good measure.

In the living room, Chiun said, "That woman is a liar."

"Why? What did she say to us?"

"She said these were very valuable coins. But there are many that are more valuable. Doubloons, pieces of eight, they are all worth more than these. Still, these are not bad."

"Chiun, stop that, will you please?"

In the hallway outside Sashur's apartment, Remo and Chiun were met by two overweight middle-aged men puffing down the hall from the elevator.

"Kaufperson," one panted. "Do you know where her apartment is?"

"Sure. Why?" said Remo.

"Police business, buddy," said the other man, his chest heaving from the strain of the twenty-foot run from the elevator.

Remo pointed to the door. "That's her apartment."

The two men ran past him.

"But you won't find her there," Remo said.

They stopped at the door.

"Why not?"

"I saw her leaving five minutes ago. She had a suitcase with her."

"Did she say where she was going?"

"She did as a matter of fact," Remo said. "I live just down the hall there. She came into to borrow some shoe polish. She's got this thing about shiny shoes. Uses only Kiwi and she was . . ."

"Get to it, man. Where was she going?"

"She said she was flying to Spokane, Washington. To see her folks. Old Mother and Father Kaufperson and all the little Kaufpeople."

"We better call the captain," one detective said. The heaving of his chest was beginning to subside.

"C'mon, fellas, why don't you tell me what this is all about. Maybe I can help," Remo said.

"Did you see the news tonight?"

"No," said Remo.

"No," said Chiun. "But I saw 'As the Planet Revolves'. It was very good today. Rad Rex is getting better and better since I have taught him how to move."

125

The two detectives glanced at each other. "Anyway on the news there was this story about this general who said there were two assassins around from the CIA. A white guy and an Oriental. And Kaufperson called and said they were coming after her. We're here to protect her."

"I guess she decided to run away," Remo said. "A white man and an Oriental, you say?"

"Right."

"We haven't seen anybody like that around here, have we?"

"No," said Chiun. "I have seen no Oriental and you have seen no white man."

"Let's go, Fred. We better call the captain."

"Yeah."

The two detectives ran back toward the elevator, while Remo and Chiun went to the exit door leading to the stairwell.

As he went into the doorway, Remo leaned back into the hall. "A white man and an Oriental, you say?"

"Yeah," said the one called Fred, impatiently jabbing the elevator button again.

"You heard about them on the news?" said Remo.

"Right, right."

"If we see them, we'll be sure to call you."

"Thanks."

Remo and Chiun went up to the roof, then to an adjoining building and down the stairs.

They met a second pair from the world of officialdom outside that building.

"Watch this, Chiun," said Remo with a smile.

Remo approached the two men, who wore trenchcoats and snap-brim hats.

"If you're looking for Sashur Kaufperson, she's gone to Spokane, Washington," Remo said.

The older of the two men turned toward Remo. "Strange you should ask, mister," he said. His partner backed away from him, moving off to Remo's right side.

"Why strange?" said Remo, looking over his shoulder and winking at Chiun, who shook his head sadly.

"Because we're not looking for her. We're looking for you."

The agent pulled his hand from his trenchcoat pocket. In it was an automatic pistol. He pointed it at Remo at exactly the same instant that his partner's gun was pointed at Chiun.

"What happened, Remo?" asked Chiun.

"I don't know. I thought I was going good."

"That'll be enough talk," said the agent covering Remo. "You two are under arrest. You're coming with us."

"A little problem there," Remo said.

"Yes. What's that?"

"I don't want to."

"You don't have much choice," the agent said. He nodded toward his gun.

"True," said Remo. "Have I ever shown you the golden triangle?"

"Don't try bribing us."

His partner added angrily, "Don't you know that in fifty years no FBI man has ever been bribed?"

"I didn't know that. Fifty years?"

"Yes. Fifty years."

"Well, I wouldn't try to bribe you. I just want you to watch. You see, it's all in the feet."

127

Remo looked down at his feet and crossed his right foot over his left foot at the ankles. "That's the starting position," he said.

"Come on, pal. You're going with us."

"Wait. I'm not done. How am I doing, Little Father?"

"For a fool playing foolish games, you are doing very well."

"Now from this point of the crossed feet, the spin is next," Remo said.

He spun on his feet, turning his body in a wide semi-circle. The agent with his gun on Remo followed the lower half of Remo's body, gun aimed at Remo's midsection. Then Remo moved at the waist. As the lower half of his body finished the semi-circular movement, the top half of his body kept twisting around, then moved forward toward the agent.

One moment, the agent had the gun; the next he had an empty hand, and Remo had recrossed his feet, spun again and was gone.

"Where. . .?"

"Behind you, Harry," called his partner.

"It's a mistake," said Remo, "to do it fast. Slow is the key. Slow, sure, precision." As Harry turned toward Remo behind him, Remo went a third time into the spin. The legs rotated, the upper body moved even farther through the turn, dipped low, moved forward and Harry's partner felt, rather than saw, the pistol disappear from his hand, and then Remo was walking off toward Chiun, both guns in his hands.

"Ridiculous," said Chiun. "You take a great secret from the ages of Sinanju and play with it on a street corner like a toy."

"Yeah, but it was good practice," said Remo. "In case I ever come up against anybody good."

"Hey you two," the two FBI agents called. "Come back here and give us our guns."

"Give them back their guns, Remo. They probably have to pay for them themselves."

"Good thinking, Chiun. Here." Remo pulled the clips from the automatics and dropped the weapons into a waist-high litter basket on a utility pole and the clips through a sewer grating.

Behind them, they heard the agents running. But by the time the FBI men had retrieved their weapons, Remo and Chiun were gone, down into a subway entrance, where Remo stopped to buy the bulldog edition of a morning paper at the newsstand.

He opened it to page three and was confronted with pen and ink sketches of "Two Secret Agents Hunted as Assassins?"

"Next you will tell me that is supposed to be me?" said Chiun.

"None other."

"Hah. Where is the joy? The love? The wisdom? The true inner beauty?"

"Shhhh, I'm reading. This general says we're probably assassins for some secret organization. The paper says it's the CIA."

"Well, see, there is some good to be found in everything. Even though that picture looks nothing like me, it is good that Sinanju is at last getting some recognition."

"That ninny general held a press conference to talk about this."

"A press conference." Chiun mused a moment. "It is a good idea. Think of the work we could get, Remo, if others knew more of us and our availability."

"Yeah, but this general blamed Kaufmann's death on us."

"Who?" said Chiun.

"Kaufmann. The guy at the Army post."

"But he was killed by gun shots."

"Right," said Remo.

"Don't they know that we would not use bullets?" Chiun's voice explored the depths of outrage.

"Guess not."

"That is a terrible thing that general did," said Chiun. "Some may see this and believe it."

Remo and Chiun walked up the steps leading to the street on the other side of the subway platform.

"This makes things tough," Remo said.

"When things get tough, the tough get things."

"What?" said Remo, folding up the paper.

"It is something like that. I heard your president say it. 'When things get tough, the tough get things.'"

"Yeah. Well, we've got a problem. Those pictures in the paper. Exposure by that nit general. We're going to have a goddam posse of bounty hunters after us next."

"Do not worry. No one will recognize me. Not from that drawing, which is not at all like me."

"And me?" asked Remo.

"You have no problem either," said Chiun.

"No? Why not?"

"All you whites look alike. Who can tell you from anybody else?"

130

CHAPTER TEN

"You're doing wonderfully, Smitty. Have you ever thought of taking an early retirement?"

"Now, Remo . . ."

" 'Now, Remo,' my ass. Yesterday, the Justice Department sent out a bulletin on us. Now, the general. All night we've been on television and in the papers. When do you have us booked for 'The David Susskind Show'? Why are you telling me not to worry? What the hell's gotten into you?"

"The pictures don't look anything like you," said Smith. "And frankly, I misjudged. I didn't think that General Haupt would fight back."

"Well, I've got news for you. General Haupt has brought great unhappiness into my life. I'm going to bring some unhappiness into his. First chance I get."

"We'll cross that bridge when we come to it,"

Smith said blandly. "The first thing is the kids. Have you found out anything?"

"Warner Pell. It was his plan."

"Then why did one of his own children kill him?" Smith asked.

"Well, Pell had this woman in it with him. Sashur Kaufperson. When the heat got put on, he was going to hand her up, and she convinced one of the kids to splat him."

"What kind of name is Kaufperson?"

"It's got one N. It's German. Two N's are Jewish."

"That's not what I mean. I never heard a name like Kaufperson."

"It used to be Kaufmann. Her husband was one of the witnesses that got zapped."

"Where is she now?"

"I've got her under lock and key. Don't worry about it."

"All right," Smith said. "Stay where you are. I'll get back to you."

"You might just sky-write the message," said Remo. "Now that everybody knows about us, secrecy isn't important anymore."

"I will call you," Smith said coldly and hung up.

Remo dropped the phone into a waste basket and turned toward Chiun, who was unrolling his sleeping mat in the center of the floor.

"Remo, please move that couch away."

"It's not in your way. You've got enough room to lay down a field of corn."

"Its presence intrudes upon my thoughts," said Chiun. "Please move it."

"Move it yourself. That's laborers' work."

132

"Hold. Hold. Are we not co-equal partners by order of Emperor Smith?"

"Chiun, he's not an emperor. For the thousandth time."

"The House of Sinanju has worked for emperors for centuries. He contracts with us; he is an emperor." Satisfied with the logic of this, Chiun demanded again: "Answer. We are co-equal partners?"

"Why does our being co-equal partners wind up with my having to move the furniture."

"It is share and share alike," Chiun said. "I am preparing my bed. That is my share. You move the furniture. That is your share."

"Right," said Remo. "Share and share alike. You go to sleep, and I move furniture. Okay. Got any pianos you want carried downstairs?" He bent over the edge of the couch and put his hands on the top of the arm. He slid the sofa back and forth to get a sense of its mass and its balance. "Move furniture," he mumbled. "Find out who's doing the killing. Find out who's behind the kids. Get my picture on television. Take out the garbage. Get rid of the bodies. I don't mind telling you that I'm getting tired of all this."

He pressed down on the arm of the couch with both hands, applying slightly more pressure with his right palm. The end of the couch tilted up into the air and Remo gave it a push. On its two closest legs, the couch skidded across the floor, like the prow of a speedboat cutting through waves. It skidded past a chair, then the parting extra pressure of Remo's right hand caused the couch to veer around the chair. It moved onward toward the wall. It slowed. Its front end lowered.

133

It dropped and stopped an inch from the wall, its left arm exactly parallel to the wall.

"Games. Always games you must play," said Chiun, smoothing out his mat.

"Furniture moving's no game," Remo said. "From now on, move your own couches."

"I will. I will. From now on, I will move the couches. You take care of the chairs. That is co-equal, right? Therefore, please move that chair. It . . ."

"I know, it intrudes upon your thoughts."

Remo lifted the chair in his arms and tossed it across the room. It landed solidly on the back of the couch and rested there.

"You, Smitty, this job—you're all getting under my craw."

"That is good. Dissatisfaction with one's lot shows that one is coming of age and is no longer a child. Think, Remo," Chiun said with sudden glee. "One day, instead of being a stupid, wilful, stubborn, insignificant child . . ."

"Yeah."

"You will be a stupid, wilful, stubborn, insignificant man. Some things one never outgrows." Chiun giggled as he delivered this last, and stretched himself out on the woven grass mat. "Heh, heh," he mumbled to himself. "Some things one never outgrows. Heh, heh."

Remo looked around the room. He saw the telephone in the wastepaper basket and put it back onto the hook.

"I'm putting the phone back on the hook," he said.

"What you do with your playthings is no concern of mine."

134

"Smith is supposed to call," Remo said. "He may call late."

"Tell him I am sleeping."

"He won't be calling for you. But won't the ring wake you up?"

"Not if I do not choose to let it."

"Hmmmpppph," Remo said.

"Hnnnnnnkkkkkk," responded Chiun, snoring deeply already.

Remo turned the bell of the telephone up to loud and wished it could go louder.

"Hnnnnnnkkkkkkkk."

Remo lay down on the couch, his head jammed against the chair.

"Hnnnnnnnkkkkkkkk." Chiun's snoring reverberated through the room. The venetian blinds seemed to vibrate from the air disturbances with little whirring sounds, like saxophone reeds.

When the telephone rang, it rang with a piercing blast. Remo jumped up on the couch, exploded from sleep by the clarion screech.

"Hnnnnnnkkkkkk." Chiun snored.

"Braawwwwkkkk." The phone rang.

"Hnnnnkkkkkk."

"Braaawwwww."

"Hnnnnnnnnnkkkkkkkk."

Fugue for Ma Bell and Adenoids. But Chiun seemed to be winning. Remo answered the phone.

"It's okay now. My wife is out."

"Remo?"

"Of course, Remo."

"No go with Warner Pell," Smith said.

"What do you mean no go?"

"He wasn't running the operation."

"Why not?" Remo asked.

135

"His total worth in the world was $19,000. Hardly what you'd expect for the head of a multimillion-dollar hit machine."

"How...?" Remo started to ask, and then changed his mind. He knew how. Smith and his computers and his inputs and his outputs and his grain movements and his shipping records and his studies of mass movements of money and his files on everybody, it seemed, who ever drew a breath, that's how. Smith knew everything. If he said no to Warner Pell, it was no.

And it was also a pain in the ass.

"Now what?" Remo said.

"I think you ought to go back to this Kaufperson person and find out more from her. She may have known who Pell's boss was. And, remember, it's somebody with contacts in the Justice Department, or they couldn't find out where the witnesses are being sheltered."

"All right," said Remo. "But I want to tell you something. When I signed on for this job, I didn't sign on to be a detective. I signed on to do my specialty, zip, zip and get out. And now I'm a detective and I don't like it. I didn't even want to be a detective when I was alive."

"Please, Remo, we're on an open line."

"I don't care. I'm tired of working out of my function. I've been a bodyguard and a messenger and a detective and I'm not supposed to be any of those things. Why don't you hire a detective if you want a detective?"

"Because good detectives cost money and you work cheap," said Smith, and before Remo could decide whether or not Smith was indulging in a rare moment of levity, Smith had hung up the phone.

Remo hung up too, vowing that the next day he would buy a new wardrobe. He would buy three new wardrobes. He would throw away all his clothes and buy enough clothes for the entire backcourt of the New York Knickerbockers, and he would charge them all to Smith.

This prospect gave him sixty seconds of unalloyed pleasure until he remembered he had done just that the week before.

"Hnnnnnkkkkkkkk." The snoring gave him no pleasure.

Remo picked up the phone again and dialed the desk.

"Desk."

"Hello, this is Mr. Maxwell in Room 453. I need a favor."

"Yes sir, I'll try."

"Are you on duty all night?"

"Yes, sir."

"Fine. I want you to ring my phone every hour. Ring it just three times and hang up. Don't bother waiting for an answer."

"But . . ."

"You see, I'm working on this big project and I've got to keep at it all night long, but I'm afraid I might doze off."

"Oh. I see, sir. Certainly, I'll take care of it."

"Fine, and in the morning, I'll take care of you."

"When should I start?"

"It's ten to twelve. Why not at midnight and then every hour from then on? Three rings."

"Very good, sir. And good luck."

"Good luck?" asked Remo.

"With your big project."

"Oh, that. Thanks."

Remo changed his shirt and as he was leaving the room, he closed the door gently behind him, holding it open just slightly.

"Hnnnnnkkkkkkkk."

The telephone rang.

Braawwwwkk.

Braawwwwkk.

Braawwwwkk.

Three rings. Remo put his ear to the door and listened.

The phone stopped. He listened. There was no more snoring.

Remo pulled the door tightly shut and walked away down the hall whistling. How did people live before there were telephones?

Sashur Kaufperson was gone. The jammed closet door had been opened from the outside by some kind of tool, probably a crowbar.

Remo began rummaging through the drawers in Sashur's bedroom. Nothing, unless one had a letch for panties with the days of the week on them and with men's names on them and with hearts on them and obscene drawings on them. Dozens of pairs of panties.

Sashur's closets were similarly unproductive. No pieces of paper left in jackets. No handbags crammed full of informational goodies. A zero.

"Why doesn't this woman write anything down?" Remo mumbled. He looked around the room. Suddenly he sensed that it was one o'clock and the telephone in his motel room was going to be ringing. Three times.

"Move your own couch next time," he growled. The telephone.

Under Sashur's telephone was a personal phone book with names and numbers and one entry that made Remo suspicious: "Walter Wilkins. Music room. Wednesday night."

It was Wednesday night.

The police department switchboard confirmed that there was a Walter Wilkins School, gave Remo the address, but cautioned that it had been closed down for several years.

It was easy to open the school's front door and even easier to find the night watchman. Remo followed the snores down to the basement where the guard slept, in a brightly lighted room, atop an old cafeteria table which was a history in wood-carving of the sexual life of the school.

Remo shook the guard awake. The guard's eyes opened wide in panic. His pupils were wide black dots. The guard saw Remo and Remo could feel the man's tension ease.

"Oh. I thought it was the head custodian." The watchman's voice was thick as he shook his head trying to clear away his sleepiness. "Who are you anyway? How'd you get in here."

"I'm looking for Ms. Kaufperson."

The guard tilted his head as if listening to something, "She's here. That's them up in the music room. The kids' chorus and her." The guard looked at his watch. "Hey, shit, it's late. I'd better tell her."

"Don't bother, buddy. I'm going up there. I'll remind her about the time."

139

Remo walked away.

"Hey. You didn't tell me who you were? How'd you get in here?"

"Ms. Kaufperson let me in," said Remo, which was not only untrue but illogical, but the guard was too tired to notice and before Remo was down the hall, he heard the guard snoring behind him.

Remo went up the dark stairwell toward the top floor. Under the soles of his Italian leather loafers, he felt the hard slate of the steps. How many years had he spent walking up the same kind of steps, in the same kind of shabby school? The orphanage school had been like this, and his first memory of it was hatred.

Every time he came down the steps in that school, he would come down hard, jumping on the edge of each step, trying to crack the heavy slate, never succeeding. At night he would lie in his metal cot in a barracks-type room full of other boys and hate the school and the nuns who ran it and the steps that were as unyielding as life itself.

No matter what Chiun thought, he had changed. If he wanted to now, he could pound the steps into gray powder. And he just didn't want to. Steps didn't matter anymore.

The closer he got to the third floor, the louder the singing became. It was street singing of the fifties, a lead singer who sounded like a castrati yodeling the high-noted melody and a background chorus that sounded like a matched set of refrigerator vibrations repeating, over and over again, one word, usually a girl's name.

"Thelma, Thelma, Thelma, Thelma." Now for our next number we will do Brenda, Brenda,

Brenda, Brenda. It was a good thing, Remo thought, that the music died before it ran out of girls' names.

He paused in the hall outside the door from which the sounds came. The windows in the door had been painted black and he couldn't see inside, but he had to admit, the kids were good. They sounded like a top-forty recording of Remo's youth.

He opened the door.

They were a top forty recording from Remo's youth.

The record was being played on a small stereo in the rear of the room which had a pile of records in position to drop and play next.

Sashur Kaufperson was at the front of the room standing at the blackboard. She wore a leather skirt and vest and a peach-pink blouse. In her hand was a pointer. The blackboard behind her was crowded with chalk writing. Remo's scanning eye picked up only scattered phrases. There were some state's names. The words "maximum sentence." Written in large capital letters were the words: Training. Performance. Silence. "Silence" was underlined.

Ten young boys sat at desks facing Sashur. Remo guessed the youngest at eight, the oldest at thirteen.

They turned toward him when he entered the room. Ten children. Children and their faces frightened Remo. They were hard cynical faces, with eyes that were blank of feeling. The room smelled of stale cigarette smoke.

The boys looked from Remo back to Sashur.

"What are you doing here?" she said, her

voice struggling to be heard over the roar of, "Thelma, Thelma, Thelma, Thelma."

"Just came to see how you were getting on. Can we talk?"

"What do we have to talk about? Your behavior tonight? Locking me in a closet?"

"Maybe your behavior. Fibbing to me about Warner Pell. Didn't you ever learn it's not nice to fib?"

"I know it. That's why I'm telling you the absolute truth when I tell you it'd be healthier if you left."

"Sorry," said Remo.

Sashur nodded slightly. Her class rose, as if on military command, and turned to face Remo. They were smiling, smiling at him, those hateful little bastards, and Remo wanted to rip them apart. He wanted to beat them, bust them, but mostly he wanted to spank them. He knew now how the nuns in the orphanage must have felt.

Again, almost in unison, their hands went into their pockets, jacket pockets, trouser pockets, shirt pockets, and they brought out pistols, small Saturday night specials.

They moved toward Remo, slowly raising their guns, like underage zombies. Remo remembered how he had frozen in the elevator when Alvin fired at him, and he did what instinct told him he should do.

He turned and ran.

The pack was after him then, silently like a pack of hunting wolves who neither bay nor howl nor yelp. Who just run.

Sashur Kaufperson stood at the blackboard as the last of the boys went out the door after Remo.

With a damp cloth, she erased the blackboard, then dried her hands on a paper towel, then walked to the back to turn off the blasting phonograph. She sighed as silence returned to the room.

A big sigh.

Remo was a man. It was a shame he had to die.

She heard the pop of shots around the corridors. Poor Mr. Winslow, she thought, remembering the custodian asleep in the basement. He never knew what went on in his school. All he knew was that Sashur Kaufperson religiously brought in a can of beer on chorus nights and poured half the can for him and stayed with him while he drank it. It gave him pleasure that an educated Jewess was his Gofor. It never occurred to him to wonder why the beer put him so quickly and deeply to sleep. He never suspected that there might be sleeping pills in the beer.

Mr. Winslow would not hear the shots, she knew.

She put on her jacket, walked to the classroom door, then remembered something.

Back at the front of the room, she picked up the chalk and wrote on the blackboard:

BOYS. BE SURE TO CLEAN UP BEFORE YOU GO.

Then she left, feeling good. It would not do for the boys to leave Remo's bullet-riddled body around where Mr. Winslow might find it in the morning and tell who was in the building.

She sighed again as she walked from the classroom.

Remo had taken a wrong turn and instead of being in a stairwell going down, he was in a stairwell that went only up. Feeling the stones under his feet, he ran to the top of the stairs.

Behind him, he heard the corridor door open again. "He's gone up," he heard a young voice whisper.

The angled stairway ended at a door. It had once had a pushbar to open it, but that was back when there had been students in the school. The pushbar was now removed and the door was locked. Remo grabbed the handle of the door and turned slowly and removed it from the metal door as easily as removing the top from a once-opened catsup bottle.

The roof smelled of a fresh tar coating, and he could feel the small pebbles imbedded in the sticky surface. A three-foot-high wall surrounded the roof. There were no stars, no moon, and the roof was as dark as the inside of an inkwell, its level surface broken only by a question-mark-shaped large pipe from an old unused ventilator system.

If Remo hid behind the pipe, it would be the first place the children would look.

Remo hid behind it. He heard the voices as the boys ran onto the roof.

"Hey," one hissed. "He's got to be hiding behind that pipe. Everybody be careful. Don't let him get your guns away from you."

Remo peered out from behind the pipe. As he did, he saw a splash of light come onto the roof from the open door. One of the boys apparently had found the light switch in the stairwell. Then the light faded as one of the boys pushed the metal door shut with a heavy clang.

Behind the pipe, Remo now heard the feet moving toward him, shuffling over the pitted roof. He heard the footsteps split into two groups and move around to come behind the ventilator from both sides.

Timing his footsteps to coincide with the soft shuffling of the boys' feet, Remo backed off from the ventilator shaft toward the far wall of the roof. He felt the railing around the roof behind him, then moved silently to his right, a dark shadow in a night of dark shadows, to the right angle corner of the railing, then back toward the center of the roof and the door that led downstairs to safety.

He was near the shedlike structure of the door when he heard the voices back in the darkness.

"Hey. Where is he? Charley, be careful, he ain't here."

The door was unguarded. Remo opened it and slipped inside, closed it softly behind him. He turned to go downstairs. Halfway down the steps was a boy, perhaps nine years old.

"Charley, I presume," said Remo.

"You're dead," Charley answered. His pistol was pointing at Remo's stomach.

It was a small-caliber weapon. Remo could take one bullet in the belly and get away with it, but the full cylinder of the gun would mincemeat him, and the knowledge of it, the galling rotten knowledge that he was about to be done in by a nine-year-old boy, made Remo angry rather than sad. He did a smooth reverse foot spin and the boy looked to the left where Remo's body had moved. But Remo was already back on the right, moving down the steps, not seeming to rush, but taking all the steps in one motion. Then he was beside the boy and the gun was ripped from the boy's hand, and Remo lifted him under one arm.

The boy screamed. Remo stuck the gun into his belt and slapped the back of the boy's head, hard, and the scream turned into a wail.

Remo stopped short. He had hit the boy. Whatever had blocked him from striking a child, he had overcome. Like a dog with a toy, he slapped the back of Charley's head again. And again.

Then he turned and still carrying the boy like a balsa log under his arm went up the stairs and toward the door leading to the roof.

"Hey, let me down. You let me down or . . ."

"I'm going to smack your head, kid," Remo said. He did. Charley cried.

Remo tossed the boy through the door onto the roof just in time for Charley to smash into three boys approaching the door, carrying them down to the roof surface.

Then Remo was low, moving through the door, and jamming it behind him so no one could escape.

As the door closed, the roof was swallowed up in darkness again. Remo opened his pupils wider than normal pupils were supposed to dilate. He could see almost as if the roof were lighted. He moved through the crowd of boys.

He slapped a face and took a gun and jammed it into his belt.

"Ooooh, shit, that hurt."

"Good," Remo said. "Try this."

He slapped again, then turned and kicked a behind and took another gun.

"Son of a bitch," the boy snarled. He was ten years old.

146

"Naughty, naughty," Remo said. He slapped the boy alongside the ear. "No cursing in school."

The boys spun around on the rooftop, like puppies looking for a hidden piece of meat that they could smell but not see, afraid to fire for fear of hitting each other, and Remo moved among them, hitting, smacking, slapping, spanking and collecting guns.

"Hey. That fucker's got my gun."

"Mine too."

"Anybody got a gun?"

Smack!

"Mustn't go calling names, big mouth," Remo said. "I'll send you to the principal's office."

"Who's got a gun?" someone cried, in a voice that bore more anguish than it was possible to experience in eleven years.

"I have," Remo said. "I've got them all. Isn't this fun?"

"I'm getting out of here. Fuck Kaufperson. Let her do her own dirty work."

"You get away from that door," Remo said, "while I put these guns away."

The biggest boy on the roof, thirteen years old, got to the door and yanked. One second he was yanking, the next instant he was sitting on the gravel-topped roof, the sharp small stones pressing into his rear.

"I said stay away from that door," Remo said. "And no peeking for the guns. That's not the way you play huckle buckle beanstalk."

Remo slipped the top grate from the ventilator shaft and dropped the small handguns in the top. He heard them slide and then thump below, as the first one landed, then the clicks as the later ones

147

landed atop other guns. He didn't know where the chute led, but wherever it ended was exactly seventeen-and-one-half feet away, his ears told him.

Behind him, he heard whispering. It was meant to be too soft for him to hear.

"The door's jammed. I can't open it."

"All right, we'll rush him."

"Yeah. Everybody jump him. Stomp him in the balls."

The boys huddled around the door as Remo walked back. They were able now to make out his silhouette even in the dark. Remo saw them as if it were light.

"Can all of you see all right?" Remo asked. "No? Let me fix that."

The boys nearest the door felt nothing except a brush of air by their faces, then they heard a thud and a ripping sound and then a splash of light as beams shone on the roof from a hole Remo had just torn open in the metal door with his bare right hand.

"There," said Remo backing up. "That's better, isn't it?" He smiled at the boys. His teeth glinted gravestone marble white in the dim light, and there was not a sound as the boys looked first at him, then at the hole in the door.

"Attention, class," said Remo, wondering how Sister Mary Elizabeth would have handled this bunch back at the Newark orphanage. Probably with a ruler across the backs of their hands, and Remo had a hunch it would still have worked. It was decades of time and social light years away from Sister Mary Elizabeth and her corporal methods of teaching, but Remo guessed that if she had had these children when they were

148

smaller, they would not now be huddled frightened on a roof with a man they had just tried to murder.

"You're probably wondering why I called you all here," Remo said. "Well, at the board of education, we've been getting bad reports on you. That you're not doing your homework. That you don't pay attention in class. Are those reports true?"

There was only sullen silence. From the darkness, Remo heard a half-whispered, "Go fuck yourself."

Remo singled out the whisperer for a blinding smile. "That's not exactly the answer I was looking for," he said, "but we'll get back to that. All right, now, what is the capital of Venezuela? Anybody who knows speak right up."

Silence.

Remo reached forward to the nearest two faces and slapped them hard, across both cheeks with his left and right hands.

"You're not trying, class. Again. The capital of Venezuela?"

A voice ventured: "San Juan?"

"Close, but no cigar," said Remo, who did not know the capital of Venezuela but knew it was not San Juan.

"All right now, all together, the square root of one-hundred-sixty-eight. Come on, don't be shy. The square root of one-hundred-sixty-eight."

He paused. "Nobody knows. Too bad. You don't know arithmetic, either. That'll have to go into my report to the board of education."

He smiled again. "Let's try grammar. Is 'walking' past tense or an infinitive?" asked Remo, who would not know either if it was mailed to him in an envelope.

"Hey, mister, can we go home?"

"Not while class is in session. What kind of child are you, wanting to miss out on your education? 'Walking.' Past tense or infinitive? Don't all speak at once."

There was deathly silence on the roof. Remo could hear only the worried shallow breathing of ten frightened boys whose decision to jump him and stomp him had evaporated when he put his bare hand through a steel door.

"I've got to tell you that this is probably the worst response I've had in all my years in the classroom."

"You ain't no teacher." It was the same voice that had told Remo to fuck himself.

"Oh, you're wrong," Remo said. "I am a teacher. True, I didn't go to teachers' college to avoid going to Vietnam. That explains why I'm not wearing jeans and peace buttons. But I'm a teacher. For instance. *You* . . . come out here."

"Me?" said the same voice.

"Yes, dummy, you." The boy, the oldest and biggest, got to his feet and shuffled slowly forward. Even with the light behind the boy, Remo could see his animal eyes, sizing up Remo, thinking maybe about a quick kick to the groin to disable Remo or at least to put him down.

"I'll prove I'm a teacher," Remo said. "Like right now, you're thinking about trying to kick me. So go ahead."

The boy hesitated.

"Go ahead," Remo said. "Here. I'll turn around. That'll make it easier."

He turned his back on the boy. The boy paused, leaned back and jumped into the air, both feet aimed at Remo in a two-foot flying kick right out of the UHF televised wrestling matches.

Remo felt the pressure of the feet coming near him, turned and leaned back just far enough so the feet stopped an inch short of his face. He grabbed both feet in his hands and dragged the boy to the edge of the roof. He tossed him over, hanging onto the struggling boy by one ankle.

When the boy realized that he was hanging, head downward, fifty feet above the pavement and that his only support might let him go if he fought, he stopped struggling.

Remo turned to the other boys. "Here's your first lesson. No matter how good you are, there's somebody better. That's true—except for one person in the world, but that doesn't matter to you. So before you get smartassed again, you better think about that. Your second lesson is that you're too young to be in this business. Now, one at a time, I think I'm going to put you over this roof so you get a taste of what dying slow is like. Would you like that, class?"

There was silence.

"I can't hear you," Remo called.

"No. No. No," came scattered voices.

"Good," Remo said. "Except you mean, 'No, sir,' don't you?"

"No, sir. No, sir. No, sir. No, sir." More voices this time. Remo looked over the edge of the roof at the boy who lay still. "I didn't hear you," Remo said.

"No, sir," the boy said. "Pull me up. Please. Pull me up."

"Let's hear you say it again."

"Please pull me up."

"Pretty please?"

"Pretty please."

"With sugar on it?"

"With sugar on it."

"Good," said Remo. He raised the boy with one simple upward move of his right hand, as if there were a yoyo attached to it instead of a one-hundred-twenty-pound boy. On the street below, he saw Sashur Kaufperson's Mercedes and realized he had been spending a lot of time on this roof.

The boy came over the railing and Remo dropped him onto the roof headfirst. The boy scurried away, crablike, afraid to get up without permission, but more afraid to stay close to that madman's feet.

"All right, class," Remo said. "Your final lesson of the evening. Every one of you bastards will be in school tomorrow morning. You're going to be nice and polite and say *yes, sir* and *please* and *thank you*. You're going to do your homework and you're going to behave yourselves. Because if you don't, I'm coming back to rip your frigging tongues out. Got it?"

"Yes, sir." The answer this time was a shouted roar.

"All right. And remember. I know your names and your schools, and I'll check on you. When I do, I hope you won't have done anything to make me mad."

"We won't. We won't, sir. No, sir, we won't."

"Good," said Remo. "And now I think it's past

152

your bedtimes and you young fellas ought to be getting home. Would you like that?"

"Yes, sir," in unison.

"All right," said Remo. He walked to the locked door.

"And just so you don't forget me."

Remo put both his hands into the hole he had smashed into the metal door, twisted his arms in opposite directions, setting up a rhythm in the metal. When it was vibrating in ways it was not made to vibrate in, he leaned back and ripped the door down its side, almost like ripping the flap off an unsealed envelope.

The roof was suddenly bathed in light. Remo stood there looking at the boys, holding the door in front of him as if it were a waiter's tray. He smiled. For the first time, all the boys could see his face clearly. He made it not a nice face to look at.

"Don't make me come after you," he said.

"No, sir." One final shout and then the boys were running down the stairs, down toward the street, and home.

Remo watched them go, then tossed the door off onto another part of the roof.

He smiled. If those kids were scared now, they should have tried lipping off to Sister Mary Elizabeth.

Remo went to the side of the building and over and down to the street. He used a light telephone wire running down the side of the building to steer himself. The wire was too light to hold his weight, but Remo did not put his weight on it, not pulling downward, but using it instead to slow him as he moved bouncingly off the wall, back to the wall, out again, each time dropping four or five feet.

Below him he saw Sashur Kaufperson getting into her Mercedes. She was pulling away from the curb when Remo got to the car, pulled open the door and slid into the passenger seat.

"Hi," he said as she looked at him in panic. "That's the one thing I always liked about teaching. The short hours."

CHAPTER ELEVEN

Sashur Kaufperson had decided to come clean. She hadn't been telling Remo the truth, the whole truth. Well, not exactly.

When she had told Remo that Warner Pell was the boss of the kids-for-killing operation, she had indulged in a slight mental reservation. Pell was *her* boss, but she knew he was not the head man. She had no idea of who the head man was.

She had been telling the truth when she said that Pell had panicked when the heat was put on and had threatened to hand her up to the authorities.

She had been shocked, stunned, frightened, but she had never entertained the thought of having one of the children kill Pell. At least not until she got a telephone call.

The caller was Pell's boss, the head of the operation. She did not know the man, who did not identify himself.

Remo groaned in disgust as Sashur kept driving.

"I have had just about enough of this almost-but-not-quite and I'm not sure and some secret voice over the phone. Who was the guy?"

"I'm coming to it, Remo," she said. "First, he told me to have Alvin eliminate Pell. He said it was the only way to save myself."

"And so at great sacrifice to yourself, and even more to Pell, you did it," Remo suggested.

"Your being sarcastic doesn't help," Sashur said.

"Gee, I'm sorry. I must have lost my manners back there when those kids were trying to kill me."

"You have to understand. I didn't train those little bastards; Pell did that. He taught them hand-to-hand fighting and weapons and other stuff. God knows what."

"And you just took roll call every morning?"

She shook her head as she made a left-hand turn.

"I'm a qualified psychologist. Pell had me work with the children on discipline, the need not to talk. I had to motivate them."

"You did great," Remo said. "I can't remember ever seeing such motivated children."

Sashur pulled the car to the curb and stomped on the footbrake.

"I'm telling you the truth," she blurted out. "Why don't you just kill me now and get this all over with? I'm too tired to hold it all in, and I'm tired of worrying. And I'm tired of trying to explain it to you without your listening."

Her shoulders heaved and her face went down against the steering wheel and she wept.

"Stop it," Remo said. "I hate women who cry."

"I'm sorry," she said and sniffled. "I'm just so tired. So tired of all this . . . the lies, the deceit, the . . . I'm so tired."

Remo patted her shoulder consolingly. "Come on. Calm down. Just tell me what happened."

She shook her head, as if splashing away tears, and began to drive again, checking carefully in her rearview mirror before pulling into the roadway.

"Anyway, I helped Pell train by doing motivation work on the children. Then one day I got a call. I told you, this was just after Pell said he was going to make me the scapegoat."

"And?"

"It was a man I never heard before. He didn't give his name. But he told me just what I was doing and what Pell was doing and then he let me know he was Pell's superior. And he told me that if I wanted Pell kept quiet, I would have to do it myself. Otherwise, I would go to jail. Oh, Remo, it made me sick. But I had to do it. I was afraid. So I told Alvin to shoot Pell."

"They listened to you? When Pell was their trainer?"

"But I was their motivation expert. They believed in me."

"And?"

"That's it," said Sashur.

"Not quite," Remo said. "What were you doing with those kids tonight?"

157

"Oh," Sashur Kaufperson said. "I nearly left out the most important part. The man who called me about Pell? Well, he called me about you and the Oriental earlier today. He told me you two would be coming, and I should have you killed. But this time I wouldn't do it. No, I wouldn't do it."

"Did you tell him that?"

"No. I just made like I'd go along with anything. But as soon as I got off the phone with him, I called the police and told them I needed protection. From you two. I thought you were killers."

"Me? A killer?" Remo asked.

Sashur smiled. "That's what I thought. And then you came to my apartment and right after that the police I had called broke in and they let me out of the closet."

"And you still don't know who this big boss is? The one who phoned you with your orders?"

"No, I do. I do. I just found out tonight."

"Who is it?"

"I saw him on television," Sashur said. "Maybe you saw him too. General Haupt. I'd know that voice anywhere."

"Good. I've got business with General Haupt," Remo said.

Remo had, of course, been aware of the car following them. The steady illumination of the interior of Sashur's car by headlights reflected in the rearview mirror, vanishing momentarily whenever they made a turn, then resuming was such a tipoff Remo hadn't even bothered to turn around to look.

So Remo was not surprised that as Sashur parked in front of his motel, the car behind them pulled around and nosed into the curb in front of them.

"Oh, balls," said Sashur.

"What?"

"It's George."

Remo saw the man getting out of the gray Chevrolet and recognized George as Sashur's boyfriend who had tried to follow them the night before, when they were leaving Sashur's apartment.

He was standing now alongside Remo's door.

"All right, you, get out of there." His voice was an attempt at a growl but too high-pitched to sound anything but playful. It was a puppy's bark.

"Sure," said Remo through the partially opened window.

Sashur restrained him with a hand on his arm. "Don't go," she said. "He's got an awful temper. George, why don't you just get out of here?"

"I'm tired of your cheating on me," George whined. Remo noticed he was a fattish man, who moved sloppily on his feet. As he talked to Sashur, he was swaying from side to side impatiently.

"Cheating on you?" she said. "Even if I were, which I haven't been . . ."

"Very good," Remo said. "Subjunctive mood. Condition contrary to fact." He turned to George. "Would a woman who was cheating on you be cool enough to say 'if I were' instead of 'if I was'?"

"If I were, which I haven't been," Sashur re-

159

peated, "how could it be cheating? We're not married."

"Name the day," said George.

"Any day but today," Remo said. "She's going out of town with me today."

"Okay, fella, that's it for you. Get out of there," George said.

"I was just coming," Remo said. He pushed open the door and moved lightly onto the sidewalk. George backed up to make room for him.

Sashur leaned across the seat to call, "Watch out for him, Remo."

Remo looked at George and saw his eyes were glistening brightly. He had tears in his eyes.

This poor nit loved that poor nit, Remo realized. Maybe they were made for each other.

"You gonna leave her alone?" demanded George.

Yes, he loved her. No doubt. Maybe she could learn to love him too.

"Make me," Remo said.

"You asked for it," George said. He threw a roundhouse right-hand punch of the variety used by brown bears to catch swimming fish.

Remo let it hit him high up on the left side of the head, moving his head just a fraction of an inch on contact. Like all noncombatants George stopped his punch as soon as it touched target. Remo felt the knuckles touch his skin, and he recoiled slightly as George pulled his hand back for another punch.

Remo leaned against the trunk of the car as if he had been knocked there.

"Had enough?" George asked.

"I have not yet begun to fight," Remo said.

George jumped forward, his body as open as a dinner invitation, and threw another right hand. Remo let this one get him on the shoulder and made a display of rolling over on the fender of the car and groaning.

"Ooooohhh."

"George, stop," Sashur yelled. "You'll kill him."

"Damn right, I'll kill him," George said. His voice was lower now, huskier. "And you too, if you cheat on me again."

"Oooooohhh," groaned Remo.

George nodded at him for emphasis and danced around to the left, throwing his left jab at air. "Want anymore, guy?"

"No, no," said Remo. "Enough for me."

"Okay. Keep your hands off my woman. This is the second time I caught you. There won't be a third time." George leaned into Sashur's car. "I'll be at the school tomorrow when you get off work. You're coming to my place and you're staying the night."

"In a pig's . . ."

"No arguments, baby. You heard me. Tomorrow after school."

Heavy-footed, George stomped away. As he drove off, he peeled rubber.

Remo waited until George's car had turned the corner before he got off the fender.

Sashur came to him. "Remo, are you hurt?"

"Never laid a glove on me." Remo touched his jaw as if it were tender. "Come on," he said, "we've got to go upstairs."

He led Sashur Kaufperson into the motel, pleased with himself for perhaps having made the

161

course of true love run a little smoother in Chicago.

Chiun was awake when they got to the room and Remo was immeasurably pleased, because he did not enjoy the prospect of waking the Master of Sinanju at 3 A.M.

The old man turned as Remo and Sashur entered. He had been standing at the window, looking out.

"Oh, Remo," he said. "I am glad you are here. Safely."

Remo squinted. "Safely? Why safely?"

"This is a terrible city."

"Why? Because it's not Persia where people like us are appreciated?"

"No. Because there is terrible violence," Chiun said. "Just now, for instance. I saw two men fighting out in the street. A terrible battle. A fat man was pummeling a skinny one into mush. Awful. Terrible. The skinny man took a terrific beating. I do not know how he was able to survive it."

"All right, Little Father, knock it off," Remo said.

"And I was so frightened. I thought, Remo might come home any moment and he might be attacked by these two terrible warriors, and I worried so. I am glad you brought this woman to protect you. She is the woman of the gold coins."

"Right. This is Sashur Kaufperson," Remo said.

"How do you do?" said Sashur, who had been watching the conversation from just inside the motel suite door.

"Sashur Kauf is a very strange name," Chiun said.

162

"It's not Kauf. It's Kaufperson," Remo said.

"There is no such name as Kaufperson," Chiun said. "Never had I heard it, even on the picture box where the names have all forms of foolishness such as Smith and Johnson and Jones and Lindsay and Courtney."

"It's Kaufperson," Sashur said.

"I suppose you cannot help it."

"I'm glad you're up, Chiun," Remo said. "I'm going to call Smitty, and then we've got to get ready to go."

"Where are we going?"

"Back to Fort Bragg."

"Good," said Chiun. "Anything to get away from this violent city. Oh, you should have seen the battle. Epic. First the fat man threw a most fearsome punch. It was like this." Chiun waved his right arm around him like a stone on the end of a string.

"Frightening," Remo agreed.

"It hit the stupid man . . ."

"Wait. Why stupid?" said Remo.

"One can tell. Even at a distance. A pale piece of pig's ear is a pale piece of pig's ear. The blow hit the stupid man alongside the head. It would have scrambled his brains, had he any."

Chiun jumped back, as if shadow boxing.

"The fat man continued on the attack with another brutal blow. Oh, the damage it would have done had it too landed on the head. But fortunately the stupid man took the blow on his shoulder. He surrendered instantly."

"Not a moment too soon, I guess," Remo said.

"He might have suffered permanent injury if he continued," Chiun said. "His hamburger eating

163

apparatus might have been broken. The physical centers that control his sloth, his ingratitude, his selfishness might even have been injured, and how then could a white man carry on in life?"

"You're right, Little Father. This is a violent city, and we have to leave. I'll call Smith."

But when he looked for the telephone atop the desk, he could not find it.

"Chiun. Where's the telephone?"

"The what?" said Chiun, turning again to the window.

"The telephone."

"Oh. The instrument that *brawks* through the night when elderly people are trying to gain a few moments of god-sent rest from the travails of the day? The instrument that interferes with . . ."

"Right. Right. Right, Chiun, right. The telephone."

"It is no more."

"What'd you do with it?"

"I suffered its intrusion upon me the first time. The second time I decided to end its *brawking* misery."

"And?"

"It is in the wastepaper basket," Chiun said.

Remo looked into the wicker basket. In the bottom of its white plastic liner was a pile of dull blue dust, all that was left of a powder blue Princess phone with touch-tone dialing.

"Good going, Chiun."

"I did not ask it to ring. I did not telephone the servant below and ask him to ring the telephone at certain intervals."

"Oh," said Remo.

"Indeed 'oh.' One who would do that should be beaten up in the street."

"May I sit down?" asked Sashur Kaufperson, who was still standing just inside the door.

"Sure," said Remo. "The chair's over there. On top of the couch. But don't get too comfortable."

"Why not?"

"You're going with us. To see General Haupt."

CHAPTER TWELVE

So it was, that without notifying Dr. Smith, Remo, Chiun, and a reluctant Sashur Kaufperson headed for Fort Bragg, North Carolina. They arrived in a rented car in mid-morning, and the new army military policeman at the entrance to the post, deciding that the hard-faced white man and the elderly Oriental that General Haupt had labeled as secret assassins were obviously not the same as a hard-faced white man, an elderly Oriental, and a good-looking woman with big boobs, waved them through after only a perfunctory look at Remo's identification which listed him as a field inspector for the Army Inspector General's Office.

They found General William Tassidy Haupt inside a field house, where he was inspecting his troops for the benefit of the photographer for the post newspaper, this being Clean Uniform Month in the new army.

General Haupt stood inside the big barn-like building, facing a line of forty men. A small squad held M-16s at the ready. Clusters of grenades were clipped to their belts. Another squad held rocket launchers. Next to them were four men holding flamethrowers.

"I think you men with the flamethrowers ought to get on the other end," General Haupt called out. He wore an immaculate khaki gabardine uniform. His trouser legs were tucked into the tops of his highly polished airborne boots. On his head he wore a white helmet with two gold stars stenciled on it. On his side he carried a .45 pistol in a brown leather holster that matched exactly the color of his boots.

"We get better symmetry if we've got the tall flame-tossing junk at one end and the tall rocket things at the other end," he said.

The four men with flamethrowers dutifully moved to the far right side of the line. The major in charge of the squad wondered if he was being moved to get him into a position from which he could easily be cropped from the picture. What had he done, he wondered. He would have to keep an eye on General Haupt, just in case he had somehow made the general's crap list.

In the center of the forty-man line stood assorted squads with hand weapons, two-man bazookas, mortars, rifles, and automatic weapons.

The captain in charge of a four-man bazooka detail said, "General, should we get on an end too?" The major from the flamethrowers smiled to himself. That's why the other officer was only a

167

captain, volunteering to put himself in a bad position.

"No," replied Haupt. "Stay where you are. This way we've got a tall element at one end of the photo and a tall element at the other end and a semi-tall element in the center. That lends balance to the picture. I think it's going to turn out real well."

"Major, how long are we going to have to hold these heavy things?" a master sergeant, sweating under the load of a flamethrower, asked the major.

"Don't worry, corporal. It's just a few more minutes and we'll have you right back at your personnel desk."

"I hope so," pouted the sergeant. "It's sergeant, sir, not corporal."

"Right. Sergeant."

"I don't know why I get all these details anyway," the sergeant said.

"For a very simple reason," the major said. "You're six feet tall and you weigh one-hundred-ninety pounds. The general wants people just that size for this picture. Sort of a Graeco-Roman ideal. There's a good chance this picture might be used across the country. Billboards. Recruiting posters."

"If it is, do I get residuals and modeling fees?" asked the sergeant.

"Afraid not. This is the Army."

"I'm going to ask the union anyway," the sergeant said.

"All right, men," General Haupt called, facing the line of troops. "Time to look alert now."

General Haupt turned to the man from the post

168

newspaper, a corporal in gabardine uniform who stood holding an old Speed Graphic camera.

"How does that look?" the general asked.

"Fine."

"What are you going to shoot at?"

"I thought F 5.6 at a hundredth."

"I don't think there's enough light in here for that," said General Haupt.

"Well, I've got slave strobe units on both ends of the line."

Haupt mused for a moment. "Yes, Corporal, that might do it. But be sure and shoot a couple at a fiftieth too."

"Yes, sir."

"All right. How do you want us?"

"I'd like to shoot from behind you, General, at the line of men."

"Will you be able to see me?" asked Haupt.

"Part of your profile," the photographer said.

"Okay. Then shoot from my left side. My left profile's better."

"Hey, general," called a voice from the ranks. "Is this almost a wrap? This rifle is getting heavy."

"Yeah," came another voice. "I've got to work out the PX entertainment schedule for the next week. I can't stay here forever."

"Almost ready, men. Just stay with it a while."

Remo, Chiun, and Sashur stood inside one of the large double doors of the fieldhouse, watching the troops shuffling into the right positions.

"Is that him?" Remo asked Sashur.

"That's him. I'd recognize that voice anywhere."

"All right," Remo said.

"Carefully, my son," said Chiun.

Remo walked across the highly polished basketball floor of the fieldhouse to the general and stood behind him. The photographer, eye to his viewfinder, swore. Who was this person breaking up his picture just when he had it composed correctly?

"General Haupt," said Remo.

The general turned. The look of concerned alert vibrancy that he had carefully constructed on his face for the photographer's benefit disappeared.

"You," he said.

"Right. Me. A little matter about murders."

Haupt looked at Remo's face for a moment, then jumped back. He grabbed the camera from the photographer and threw it at Remo. If he got him, that would do it. He knew that kind of camera would hurt, because once he got hit by an Associated Press .35mm camera with a .235 millimeter telephoto lens, and it was real heavy because it went down to F 2.8.

The camera missed.

"Use your men," Sashur Kaufperson shouted from the corner of the room where she had sidled away from Chiun and stood watching.

But General Haupt had already thrown the only weapon he knew how to use. He began to back away from Remo. Over his shoulder, he called to the major at the end of the line:

"Call someone from a combat battalion."

"The combat battalions are off for the day, General," the major yelled back. "Remember, you gave them the day off for finishing second in the inter-Army shoe shining contest?"

"Oh, yeah. Hell," said Haupt.

170

He was now backed against the wall. Remo stood in front of him.

"Use your troops," Sashur Kaufperson yelled again.

"Troops," General Haupt yelled. "Protect your commander." He got those words out just as Remo dug a thumb and two fingers into Haupt's collarbone area.

Back in the line, the major with the rocket launchers asked the captain next to him "Do you think we should call the police?"

The captain shrugged. "I don't know if the police will come on the post. Federal property, you know." He turned to a young lieutenant from the judge advocate's office who stood in combat infantryman's garb, holding an M-16.

"Freddy, can the city police come onto the post?"

"Not without express permission from the commander."

"Thanks." The captain looked at General Haupt, who was writhing against the wall, his face contorted in pain.

"I don't think he'd want to sign a paper now inviting the city police in."

"No, I don't think so," the major agreed. "Maybe we could call the Marines. Marines are federal."

"Yes, but the nearest Marine base is far away. They couldn't get here in time."

General Haupt was on the floor now. Remo knelt alongside him.

"I wish violence was my classification," the lieutenant from the judge advocate's office said. "I'd like to put a stop to this."

"Yes," said a captain in the middle of the line. "I would too but I don't know how human relations would apply to this situation." He was a psychiatrist.

A lieutenant with a mortar suggested wrapping Remo up in telephone wire. He was in communications.

The major at the end said, "Perhaps we'd better wait for further orders."

The officers nodded. "Yes. That's probably best," the captain said. He felt sorry that there was nothing in the manuals to cover this situation.

Remo knew something that wasn't in the manuals either. He knew that when you wanted to get someone to talk, fancy wasn't important. Pain was. Any kind of pain, inflicted any way you wanted. Beat them with a stick. Kick them on the knee until it was puffed and bruised. Anything. Make them hurt, and they would talk.

He was inflicting pain now upon General William Tassidy Haupt, but the general was still not talking to Remo's satisfaction.

"I tell you I don't know anything about any children killer squads," he gasped. "The Army's minimum recruiting age is eighteen."

"They're not in the Army," Remo said, twisting the bunched mass of nerves just a little tighter.

"Ooooh. Then what would I have to do with them? Why did you pick me?"

"That woman over there. She identified you." Remo jerked his head toward the door.

Haupt squinted. "What woman?"

Remo turned. Sashur Kaufperson was gone.

172

Chiun was walking slowly toward the line of troops.

"Well, she *was* there," Remo said.

"Who is she? What branch is she with?"

"She's not with any branch. She's with the school system in Chicago."

"That settles it then," said General Haupt. "I don't know any school teachers in Chicago. I haven't even talked to a school teacher for twenty-five years."

Remo twisted again and Haupt groaned.

"You're telling the truth, aren't you?"

"Of course, I'm telling the truth," Haupt said.

Remo looked at the general, then let him go. He knew nothing. And it meant that Sashur Kaufperson had lied to him again.

He left the general lying on the floor and turned back to the line of troops. Chiun was walking up and down the line, inspecting uniforms, straightening a pocket flap on one soldier, adjusting the field cap of another.

"Shoes," he said to the lieutenant from the judge advocate's office. "Your shoes could be shined better."

"Yes sir," the lieutenant said.

"Take care of it before we meet again," Chiun said.

"Chiun. You about ready?" Remo asked.

"Yes. I am done. This is a nice army." He turned back to the line of troops. "You have beautiful uniforms. The nicest army since the Han Dynasty. You look very good."

Remo took Chiun's arm and steered him away.

"Chiun, where is Sashur?"

"She said she went to the persons' room."

173

"She lied."

"Of course, she lied," said Chiun.

"Why didn't you stop her?"

"You didn't tell me to stop her," Chiun said.

Remo shook his head. "Did you ever think of enlisting? You'd go far."

"I do not like armies. They solve problems by killing many when the solution to all problems is to kill one. The right one."

The MP at the gate told Remo, yes, sir, he had seen the woman leave, sir. A man in a car had come up to the gate, looking for her, had driven inside, and a few minutes later had left with the woman, sir.

"Who was the man?" Remo asked.

"Heavyset man. I took his name down. Here it is. George Watkins, sir. From the Justice Department."

"What'd you say?" Remo asked.

"From the Justice Department. He had credentials."

"Thanks," Remo said, driving past the guard booth. It all came together now. George. The Justice Department leak.

"Where are you going?" Chiun asked.

"After George."

"If he beats you up again, do not look to me for help."

"Hmmmppphhhh," Remo grunted.

CHAPTER THIRTEEN

Remo's rented blue Ford caught up with George's rented green Ford two miles from the Army post.

As he drove up close behind George's car, Remo saw Sashur Kaufperson sitting in the front passenger seat swivel her head around continuously, watching Remo as if she were wishing he would somehow vanish.

Remo planted himself right behind George and began to blow his horn.

George turned to look. Remo motioned him to pull over. Sashur, with her left hand, turned George's head forward to look at the road. With her right hand, she gave Remo the finger. Up close, he could see her well. Her mouth was working, sputtering. He could imagine the words pouring out of it.

"Hold tight, Chiun," Remo said, as he swerved

left to pull out around George's car on the narrow two-lane road.

"No," said Chiun. "Hold tight is wrong. Loose is the secret to safety. Loose. Free to move in any direction."

"All right, already," said Remo. "Hold loose if you want to."

He was alongside George's car now, riding on the left side of the road. Again he leaned on his horn and began motioning to George to pull to the side of the road.

He saw Sashur Kaufperson's right hand come up slightly to hold the bottom of the steering wheel in George's hands. Then she gave the wheel a strong counter-clockwise twist. George's car swerved sharply to the left, just as Remo feathered the brake with his toe. George's car shot across the road in front of Remo, hit a low steel guard rail, and bounced along the rail for fifty feet before rolling to a stop.

Remo pulled his car in behind George, but before he could even turn off his key, George was out of his car, stomping angrily back toward Remo.

He stopped outside Remo's door.

"All right," he said. "I've warned you for the last time. Get out of there."

"Is there anyone you wish me to notify, Remo?" asked Chiun.

Remo growled and shoved open his door. It hit George square in the midsection and drove him backward over the guard rail. He landed on his shoulders in a small patch of roadside tiger lillies. He got heavily to his feet.

"That's not too smart, buddy," he said. "You'll pay for that."

"George," said Remo. "I want you to know that I think you're an asshole."

"Yeah?"

"Yeah."

"Is that right?"

"That's right."

"Who says so?" demanded George.

"You work for the Justice Department, don't you?"

"That's right, and you better not fool around with me, pal."

"And you know where the Justice Department is hiding out its big witnesses, don't you?"

"That's none of your business, buddy," said George heatedly.

"And for a little nookie, you spill it to that leather-lunged bitch in your car . . ."

"Hold it. Hold it right there," George said. "I don't have to . . ."

"Yes, you do," said Remo. "I just want you to know *why* you're going to die." Behind him Remo heard a car's engine racing. "And do you know she's been killing off the government's witnesses?"

George laughed. "Sashur? My Sashur? Killing witnesses? Really, fella. Now that's too much. Sashur is the kindest, sweetest, most gentle . . ."

"George," said Remo. "You're too stupid to live."

Behind him Remo heard a car pull away. In front of him, George went into a shoulder holster to pull out an automatic.

Between removing the weapon from his holster and getting it into firing position, an unusual

177

thing happened to George. He died as Remo jumped over the guard rail with an elbow thrust that carried George's enlarged stomach organs before it and mashed them against George's backbone.

"And besides," Remo said, looking down at George's corpse, "you annoy me."

"Good, Remo," called Chiun through the open door of the car. "I was afraid he might beat you within an inch of your life."

"Oh, blow it out your ass," mumbled Remo.

He looked at George's body, lying like a large mound alongside the road, and realized he couldn't just leave it there. It was certain to be spotted and to draw attention, so Remo lugged the body back, over the guard rail and shoved it into the rear seat of his car.

He got behind the wheel, and Chiun pointed a long-nailed finger at the windshield. "She went thataway," he said.

"Thanks, co-equal podner."

Remo found Sashur's car three-quarters of a mile down the road, where the narrow two-lane blacktop road had widened into a four-lane divided highway. The green Ford was parked alongside the highway and was empty.

As he sat in his car behind the other auto, wondering where Sashur had gone, Remo saw a state trooper's squad car go by in the opposite direction.

In the back seat was Sashur Kaufperson. As the squad car passed Remo, she turned and looked out the rear window and gave Remo the finger again. And a victorious smile.

Then, with a whoop of its sirens, the squad car was off down the road at high speed.

After Remo had followed the car to a nearby hospital, into which a smiling Sashur was aided by two state troopers, he called Smith.

He told him that George was the Justice Department contact and that Sashur had been in charge of the kids for the killing operation. He told Smith where she could be found, but Smith ordered him not to bother her in any way.

"Leave her to us, Remo. We should be able to get some information from her that's worth having."

"All right," said Remo. "And take care of George too, will you? He was a shmuck, but he shouldn't be left to rot in the back seat of a car."

"Leave the car in the airport parking lot. We will see to George," Smith said.

Remo hung up, but instead of feeling satisfied over a job neatly wrapped up, he felt disquiet.

He talked to Chiun about it on the plane back to Chicago.

"This is all over, completed, finished," he said.

"If you say so," Chiun said, refusing to interrupt his usual flight routine of staring at the left wing to make sure it was not falling off.

"Then why do I feel rotten about it?" asked Remo.

"It has been a complicated matter, with many ends that are loose," Chiun said.

"That's no answer," Remo said.

"Then you are not ready for an answer. When you are, you will not need me to give it," Chiun said. "I think that wing is loose."

179

"If it falls off, you can float to earth on a cushion of your own hot air," Remo said sullenly.

"Do not blame me for your ignorance," said Chiun. "There is some learning that must be done alone. No one can teach a bird to fly."

On a scale of one to ten, the consolation that thought brought Remo was a minus three. He was dissatisfied throughout the rest of the plane flight, dejected when he reached Chicago, and disgusted when he and Chiun went to Atlantic City for a rest. Chiun was overjoyed to find that Atlantic City's streets were the inspiration for the game of Monopoly, even though his joy dissipated when he passed the Boardwalk and Baltic Avenue six times in one day and no one gave him two hundred dollars.

Ten days later Remo was still down when he talked to Smith.

"Everything has been taken care of," Smith said. "Our friend George was unfortunately killed in a car accident. However, his widow will collect his Justice Pension."

"What about Sashur?" Remo asked.

"She is now in custody," Smith said.

"What's she being charged with?"

"That, unfortunately, poses a problem. We cannot try her. The publicity would tear our anti-crime program apart, and who knows how many mental cripples would try to follow her act?"

"You mean, she's getting off scot free?" Remo said in dull surprise.

"No, not exactly. Ms. Kaufperson has been very helpful to us in preparing cases against those people with whom she contracted for . . . er, work.

Many of them may be going away for a while as a result of her information."

"But what about her?"

"I don't know," Smith said. "After it's all over, maybe a new identity, a new start. Obviously, we couldn't send her to prison. With the people she's offended, she wouldn't last twenty-four hours."

"Where is she now?" asked Remo.

"The Justice people have her safely away, out of harm's reach," Smith said.

"Where?" Remo asked casually.

"She's squirreled away in a little town in Alabama. Leeds," Smith said. "And how are you do——" Smith was cut off by the click of the telephone.

Remo turned and looked across the hotel room to where Chiun sat on the threadbare carpet, meditating.

"This bird is learning to fly, Little Father," Remo said.

Chiun looked up and smiled. His hands opened and the fingers moved upward like a blooming flower.

"The blood of Sinanju runs in you, my son, as strongly as if you were born hearing the waters of the bay. When you were first attacked by those children, you could not respond because you were but a child yourself in the ways of Sinanju."

"I know," said Remo. This time he did not feel insulted when Chiun spoke of his ignorance.

"But you quickly grew," Chiun went on. "And you are growing still."

"It is a terrible thing to teach children to kill, is it not?" Remo asked.

"It is the worst of all crimes because it not only

robs the present of life, it robs the future of hope."

"I know," said Remo.

"Then you know how it must be answered."

"I do now," Remo said.

Leeds' main real estate broker was delighted to show the young man some of the property for sale in the town, but unfortunately the house on the hill overlooking the town had just gone off the market.

"Oh? Who bought it?" the young man asked.

"Fella from up north. Said he needed rest and quiet. Didn't look sick though. Heh, heh. Nothing too sick about a man who pays cash for a house."

In the house on the hill that night, Sashur Kaufperson felt good. Even though she was disgusted with Alabama television and its good old boys with their "hiyalls" and their "golly gees," and even though the Justice Department man assigned for her protection had rejected her offer of bed and bod, she felt on top of the world.

A few more sessions and she'd be clear, with some money, a passport, and a new identity. She would be off to parts unknown and eventually to Switzerland where several hundred thousands of dollars waited for her in a numbered account.

As she lay in bed listening to the crickets outside her window, she smiled. She had challenged the system and won. Free. And rich.

As she thought of all the things the future had to hold for a rich, liberated female-type person, she did not notice the crickets hush. Nor did she hear her window open quietly.

182

She only realized someone was in her room when she felt a hand clasp over her mouth and another hand move into her collarbone and press nerves that made it impossible for her to move.

"Killing is bad enough," a voice whispered to her. "But making children into killers is the worst crime of all. The punishment is death."

When he had finished her, the killer took her body into the bathroom, where he ran a bath, forced water into Sashur's lungs, and left the body crumpled in the tub.

Then as silently as he had appeared, he went out the window, closing it behind him. He moved into the deep grass, where his shadow blended with the other shadows of the night, and only the sudden stilling of the crickets marked the movement of the youngest Master of Sinanju—in that ages-old house, hardly more than a child himself.

A happy child.

ALL NEW DYNAMITE SERIES

THE DESTROYER

by Richard Sapir & Warren Murphy

CURE, the world's most secret crime-fighting organization created the perfect weapon — Remo Williams — man programmed to become a cold, calculating death machine. The super man of the 70's!

Order		Title	Book No.	Price
_____	# 1	Created, The Destroyer	P361	$1.25
_____	# 2	Death Check	P362	$1.25
_____	# 3	Chinese Puzzle	P363	$1.25
_____	# 4	Mafia Fix	P364	$1.25
_____	# 5	Dr. Quake	P365	$1.25
_____	# 6	Death Therapy	P366	$1.25
_____	# 7	Union Bust	P367	$1.25
_____	# 8	Summit Chase	P368	$1.25
_____	# 9	Murder's Shield	P369	$1.25
_____	#10	Terror Squad	P370	$1.25
_____	#11	Kill or Cure	P371	$1.25
_____	#12	Slave Safari	P372	$1.25
_____	#13	Acid Rock	P373	$1.25
_____	#14	Judgment Day	P303	$1.25
_____	#15	Murder Ward	P331	$1.25
_____	#16	Oil Slick	P418	$1.25
_____	#17	Last War Dance	P435	$1.25
_____	#18	Funny Money	P538	$1.25
_____	#19	Holy Terror	P640	$1.25
_____	#20	Assassins Play-Off	P708	$1.25
			and more to come	

TO ORDER

Please check the space next to the book/s you want, send this order form together with your check or money order, include the price of the book/s and 25¢ for handling and mailing, to:

PINNACLE BOOKS, INC. / P.O. Box 4347
Grand Central Station / New York, N.Y. 10017

☐ Check here if you want a free catalog.

I have enclosed $_____ check_____ or money order_____ as payment in full. No C.O.D.'s.

Name_____

Address_____

City_____ State_____ Zip_____
(Please allow time for delivery.)